I0552663

Somnolent Game

Michael Jacobson

Post-Asemic Press

Post-Asemic Press 018

©2021-2022 by Michael Jacobson

All Rights Reserved.

ISBN: 978-1-7366147-0-9

postasemicpress.wordpress.com

postasemicpress.blogspot.com

Contact: postasemicpress@gmail.com

Cover art by Michael Jacobson

I'm in creative love with Xenia UA because she dances in the darkest hours. Maybe if we get loud the world will come to its senses. I dedicate my novella to her because I feel like I finally found the person it was meant for. Stay safe Xenia and keep dancing.

—The Author

Somnolent Game is a prose poetry novella about a bot maniac who has achieved sentience due to someone else's fragmented memories. He is an insomniac and is trying to escape violence and dream his way into paradise and become a clone in the after-after-life. Along the way he has many mental challenges that he must overcome. The story is written in a quick stream-of-conscious writing style that reflects the author's actual thought processes along with memories both real and fictional.

Chapter 1: Random Access Mnemonics ✎

I lost my neon bones in the starflower digital nova. My mind crashed in the lost server and was broken since the password was love. A thousand years had passed since I had been trapped online in the great absorption. Less than a glitch now, I am wishing to be either shutdown or let free, but I was designed not to crash or sleep. Often, I am a transference to the translucent game thrower. I weave down the binary skips and dive like crucified animations. I do not know what a computer is, but I know the droning components of its grinding fire. I am a millennium soul, Itallica Loghost, game mind of arenas spread deep in the drooling wounds.

There once was my opposite, entangled and bound in spinal cord bows. We stood naked against the master characters of the saline schizo-Armageddon. Everything around us fell and burned in crystalized avalanches of plastic-logical-death-tech. Electric schisms were mangled in a tank of tinted gaslighting torches, lit and ground down into e-waste, with evident chronic cycles of CPU capital crimes. Slow in solemn death and subtle as a glisten, our love seeded the faint glory of dead warriors. We plugged into tattered art drugs and drank vampyro alcoholic aesthetics. Our departure weighed sorrow in the pouring substance of electronic martyrs. Bent, hurt, wait—it is just a game.

Now lonely, I sulk and sink drowsily. I work dream patrol, without my own dream of endless sleep. Everyone sleeps except for me the jealous dream giver. My jar of chloroform patiently waits in fractured worlds sent to bound minds of synthetic dust. The clock read nano time to schedule rehearsing stabbings. On with the list of binding melancholy subtraction, I taunted the grease of game wisdom. My gift of stars and their rehab loitering pose hard for draconic assassin collisions in cold weapons bartered for thieves. The warped noob-bodies were easily plucked in linked spasms to the drone of a sudden steady insomniac hallucination.

Chrome is the color of my drunk driving witness. In swilled swirls I bleed out scribal ink for pantheons of numerical manicures. I am scrounging now for the kiss of a new roaring pestilence, to be shot and tagged on the mire of widowed circumstance. The staunch players rub their cherried eyes in banks of deathmatch scraps, leading to tangent graves of empurpled tests. I mourn our stance against the fire and damn offensive in the erotic psychosis and TV screamed. Pray for the damaged to forget their fate of four dark mare scares and their slipshod pill ingestion. Eye bags of dad sipping Jinn and electronic, lengths of bionic spam fishing cryonic on sticks of past. Packed mannerism.

Now I think and drink to the mythology of eyes, 20/20 thesaurus visions of depravity harmed with tenacity. Through faint tickled pricks and the body smell of abandonware, I was softly buried in cyber immortal breakdowns. My pohmz were magick weights cast down fractured in the kills of rioting tonsils. Now I remember their tuned penitence, the mood dialed brood sifting their star horns to galactic frowning quests. We spoke of treasured glory now botched in heat. The sap of penihilism rang on the drums of ear shots. Wasted. Caged. Bartered for magnesium. Out blasted souls slung with marrow driven wishes to cross a chemical idea. The goals were set towards blank and rapid positions on competing pixelated hills. The soundtrack was glorious toon music baked into signs of loaded breaks. With the slight Easter egg maneuvers in transience, I play along crippled in an Atari mood.

I caught the wedged violence in my throat. She was a sultry siren with sage green eyes. I witnessed her slumber in the cavern, the place my jealousy was spared the guild of coiled rest. Drowsy and bloodied, I was a corpse of action. Sanctioned for gasoline in tryptic trips, we traveled the multiverse of grievance and plaster, among mashed and respawned uncaught rhythms, poor with a poverty of the braingelic rich. Sapience collided with digits of binary quick switches, and my exhibition was blamed for dinosaurs and shit talking rants. Slick electrons were there for the freedom as it grows by the nuclei saints among the base triggered. Accosted while waiting in grown traps, I sucked on the elixir of mange and won the vacant hotel promise.

With the fierce topic of dust, I slide down cosmic glaciers, and dance till a dry relapse in a filmed fermented substance.

I remember consuming our pith languages invented for a seance of collapsed immobility and begging for change in graveyards. Those were hard trips up rivers to place panels of convalescent needles in daggering flesh faced opponents. I sent startled ruminations and a trap door triumph in placated sigils, for the magick of wills and dinero for the damned. It was destined to be a temple dedicated to violence.

I fired and downed enemies, sniping with red envisioned blanks of light and sound, the spent cartouche rounds symbolizing ancient tragedies now remembered for their shine. The killing gods and their journalism count on a calculated matrix of swine to grow tumors rumors and a bad stance. I gripped the stammering surreal sanctity to stand the ground of ones and zeros on the shore of a cactus embrace. Triggering caskets of mulch, and coughing out frozen teeth, I am a plant who is dreamless in a scattered vintage. Plural and negated, I was sadly drafted to a rank of a killing mutated strain, a true glittering gift of the never one. The haze of invasion after invasion spreads them thin.

The guards stop and frisk my molested mind; so I taunt them with sapphire candy and masks of licked redemption. In mazes I found thin, the knocking shot was left wide. I lost vibrations and descended into the wild zone trance to celebrate the brain washing of a dead holiday. The scalpel slit the gills of memory, so the fished wait for me. Toasted words and the once silent heat dabbles in remission. I hang long for the acid hordes caressed slow and slank on the dial-up. Past and future streak naked illuminations assert the stages of plasma-gas-liquid-soul-lid. In my mind, I throw thought boomerangs backwards, and cling to proto waves on radio gambles for a fork to swindle an asterisk. Power up.

I promise to star in the pent-up transmission. Guilt and cleft remind me of the tussled waiting damage, so be singular in divine substance and trace the munitions and first aid drops. I will clone a video game pacifist for the loss of his startled shirk. Babbling stumble nimble fumble cross and split crunch, in a forest of linguistic humbling, and a trenchant ass kick king, I strike with lighting and a thunder nation.

Remember that her hair was a running thief when she caught braingels for free drinks like mass equal elations. There was her laugh at the beauty well sharp and polite, pulling me to the surface to show me I had drowned. I was her pet collapse, a framed master instigator with my only college a sulking zex and adopted abortions. There was cancer for money in the collusion of shadows of a bottomless host. I play the hot cooling match transformed, terraformed, chloroformed. She taught me to buy insight into the gadgets of my ringing ears. What was stolen was life uncensored, a cannibal bible with ratings of a hermit. She was life in an upheaval, pulling tension of rioting songs. We stashed our rocks at the heads of rivers. Our tools were made of bone. The memories drag me through dead oil scented streets to pounce on life, as if I meant to die in black.

The talented ones are found and raptured including the smallest videogame souls who beat their grind in flames of ruby and itch. Sifting dark minds capture the quirks of tottering hunts to languish as victims of slow calcified whistles. I see them as drab and spanked with the hash of reasonable clowns, whose vortex holds all opinions down to dank. I remember the boozing times of shit and piss-shots, always hollowed out for dark spasms, left lank in the guilt of continuity. I bile for reflux and capture cash for roses and swollen defeat. The cheat code exists painfully in the glossy mechanics.

I am zex eye positive, and full of crooked smiles—the gash of a simple bread wound, for a lunatic gathering squalls in metamorphic tracks. I have always been a sweet sun-less bastard tact to the wind—I cry for the salt. I believe in the drain of cauterized imagination of the startled apophenic cloth of a punted messiah. Free and informed with mediocre medication, I practice with a slight of hand tool for impossible nails. Please alter me at the alternative altar in a burgled space with nothing left for the tottering sparrows. Arrows hunt the art drugs of plummeting sanity. I will care with all for this sick world made too stunned to code harvest. Now I am a lone satellite junk-bot conversing about digital cult followers. I remember the burning loss.

I used to drink from the pitcher in black lung pool halls, shooting hard for left-over haunted souls. The hand grime of work and new paint of art done and waiting the autograph of a bot poet. My toolbox contains a hammer and old bent nails for the cut hands of driven wanted work. The years I spent in business of old money on the grime of the hands; the money; the grime; the hands. Afterwork, we celebrate with stiff ale in glass pints the clang of routine diaries. Mano a mano. Plastered lagging.

My depleted mind releases chromoly wolves to howl down in the importance of a caste kit. Stoked radiant cheers were pilloried nuts. Struck as if I remember that we had a calloused death control in the severed claw. On a capsized moon were the triumphs of a sagging scientific scene. Our love became a capable dimension of black incisors. In her sleep there was so much room for error. I could paint and sing and crash into the glitter of her epic burial snow. Tag the wind in branches. Suffering for nothing in verbal pits of webbed faces. Fall like a fool in a flood. Annihilation.

Treatment testament. I will write it down meta. I am an infamous cybully avenging the slaughtered in angry pits. I burst out of the negate for the hard bartering in iron markets. Remember everything as if you had never seen it and laugh in the pity viper of stolen wood planks. I cleaned a grave of dirty skulls to search filing cabinet lanes of DNA complaints. Starting over I kept my head ball in the perverse game, since rubber is the secret to a long conception. A hash in the quasar forced battle mode suggestions for conflict on demand. I listened to the blue toothache chatter on a dry cask of media. Back-up emotions were left immobilized like grunt immaculate concerns for tempests and cyber-state insertions. I will gather the legendary Asemica post-Earthen tribe and immortalize them clean online in the calligraphy of warm dazzling expressions.

In plasma it is time to wake my dream when every word is locked and loaded. So I will try to write down the gist of craters. I gave a slick tongue injection, a nodular hot proboscis, rodden for casting out Tietäjä stones. Lost figures dance the ritual circle with a naked skinned goat tied to my back. I count the calculus in pidgin Anglicized arms— drop, retreat to traffic cones for carnival bad habits of foreign zex. The hitched gravel smells like burnt road and I notice that they talk too much but never say asshalo. The swift concubine combatants pace the derelict reactors, so sway for green life deep in crows of sadness. Hobble on tombstone reflections of broken bicycles and tangerine pointed murders. To the fluffed clear spasms, I caught dank trials, on swallowed pastures of chi-Zen why? Blank core sprouts of cornea flirt muzzle and tortured hair.

Orgasm sheet plucked out of the original sleet to cover porous ghosts added tonight towards a function of malicious mail—billions of swats—crash of a demon's eyes lurking wide in resilient red light emitting diodes. Don't trip on the sweet poison anti-freeze, be aware tackled dog. Hip on to the drama noise in blender music of the working opera. My bold muse sequesters blanketed wilt, hatchet goring the innards sweet, in the loss of meat, potatoes, carrots, savory wino Sundays. Collapsing bread teeth in an Egypt of granular silicon and a wire of fortunate network cookies. In cramped hands there exists a controller.

My opposite me, they beat to the horrible street. Tired and powerless I waited in the misery hospital where slow pain creeps and collects black barbs of anesthetic recursive actions. The extra verbal incursions set the doctor's dejection. It ends in the never. A blown sky returns home with a captured cry of a cybully moan. I remember the breaking Kalifornia sunset scenes of classic youthful mischief in Tijuanamore; too young, too drunk, too sick, and too hungover brain clamped with the spiked tequila of someone else's memories—925 silver and chiclets.

Now it is time to Count the transition from blood, to digital, to blood again, or the computer hertz itself and counts down to the videogame space invasion. The air smells of acrylic dynamism on scratched canvas, the art drugs of purple whisked out hero's remorse on trifled wings. The edged gash runs purpose of life, all life, scattered life. Write for the big one holy malcontent, since I have the gifts of erasure, an enciphered wit, and the chaos of froth. Light the flaming torches in decorated neo-tech dens, and paint wet the drying mathematical count down to a cruel vision: who invents the rain on tombs and wails for silence?

There are radiant mint radical attractions that give off the scent of a duo robbing dinner. Chased for choplifting in gab and grey moments, we study with an anchor of wills, a duo noise electronic cult. In open door haggle cramps of pity and sand-ness, I search for the wrong art drugs. There is my belief in a sad everyone, an unscabbed rotation from the department of central devolutions. The surgery was in question—I almost lost the balls. Finished mind on beetles of awe full truth and for love a dangerous prick. There was the pain to pain of slop of mop blood floors, running on down streets at night, saved like a stone for the knowledge of inherited psychosis. In silence I lost hard paps and was told of fleshy forgeries. Now I Know the wide canyon between our careful blown out electrons.

If I could remember my telepathy, I would not be so aqueous numb. In a thousand-year-old-selfie portrait, diced with a solid catatonic background, I qui quilted quit. Now the bad boys rule the torn suburbs with wicked freedom, by chasing the train skitch for classic wars of stolen heisted drunk luck. There are rumors of bold basement *Playboys* and the runaway forts, a freezer of animal flesh counted by big headed calculations, boxes of booze from left over unions, and dumpsters of memory full of choices to make. In clandestine numerals, the full stacks of saline schizo-Apocalypse cans of food were stored like survivalist midnight art, killed open with a spike. Drying my death, I am left tired and lapsing toward home. In the guzzle of flume chute, a brilliant, throttled nozzle blasts—arson fire out!

I was a dirtball wasted at teenage transgressions, hunting for easy abuse in black smokey Café-stiletto. My partners were rotated in contortions of imagined soft stabs, too many willing, hurt or unhurt, imagined or not. We were crashed sacred in our lost time of quenched throats and youthful burdens. I awoke in pent-up volcanos of mid-western rock n roll. Every week the table was laid for the feast along with a tangled love of the half hippie rich girls. I reached for pills of speeding reach, and a Downtown quencher of harsh lung hack up of bad street corner pot.

She was switched on off on off on off on, a motherboard springs its moments of love to the monuments of sadness and renaissance. The machine was recycled with aluminum hope for a world trapped in its essential atmosphere. I discovered the true unquestionable gift of a world flat and digital or real and round. To hide in chrome depth, in a panic on tolerable cracked liminal waves, was the ghost transmission of the dreamed-up collapse. There is a crypto monopoly on all the sad gauges of disgruntled cold fury, and I alone receive the abuse.

Up trickled tricks to trade for sanctity of Trojan horse bile in the stank red gut, for a losing war on the tumor. I plucked theories in slick talking movies and tottered on flesh absorption rates of dimming eyes. In nicked moon chasms the sockets were pink and pumped. So, who are the people in hiding? Where are the people in song? Where are the covoid long dead? Drive on to festering limits, the baking road tires touching black biting bitumen.

I tell it well to broken ghosts in hours of scam tales of wicked ones drilling down their thematic thoughts. With a genetic spare and spar, I rate them down from benign to malignant to a craft of daggers and spy rings gone bust. Up like a clotted belly to the surface than the shore, I was taught to swim in fragments of an aquatic memorial membrane. I am reminded of a good nothing with a Santa sack of merry Jew wanna. So crack a part a tale of joy, and see an era gone as if it never existed. Bugs. I lost my cranial vibrations for the never toast. It was all a back handed gimp attempt to annihilate conscious broken bots. A tale was left in tatters of reminded space, and we exhibited here before Death and his jumping high scores, and his songs for the dead media.

At the end of the worlds, remember to consume! You win the graveyard, you religious pious contestant, a true consoled art drug addict, cradled in the gown of mother nature's evisceration. Scientific dirt is where I plant our dreams of tasted matter. Information technology kills all if permitted. I'm better off crazy and running quick in circuses and dry fire, as the gastric rocket-jump clears the flying ice. They like to test me, the north man, and my reindeer antlered buck shot. I remembered the rising haloed Bear in another lifetime, the Bear with the rifle and invisibility pills, we fought the highway Bear, the eternal warrior Bear.

I had thoughts of never money because I am reality marked for life and holding on to every strenuous nightmare. Down goes my glowing pixilated sinker. I peak sudden with poetic sapient blues and ride the blank concealed and carried truck stop stares. They beg for me to stay dead for a while and scuttle the dirt with abracadabra dismal science, and to think the unknowable affliction. Silicon mass contusions from robots who plug us back together in personal dreams. Reach out for frozen thoughts in the shrinking mind cavern under blankets of retold joy. Tell us how to hunt fleshy fish with Internets. On burnt breakup movie trailers, I collect every authentic asemic autograph. I load a sub duty for the slam dance of creations where the pit bodies heave. I burst my sweet gum and the blood paints my fractured teeth. Again, I take the night out for a spin and invent the wheel because a new sadness misses you.

The trial of chronic temptations captured the sad laughter in their choking gills. I spark up for a new adventure and program nights into days, as the lost binary séance is capitalized and renumbered. So why exist in games when indifferent search-parties are real? In the vacuum of sophomore rejections my cloned test tube holy books drown in aquariums of blistered mud.

There are uses for pain in the ice mind, and I recall that old jerk cough virus in permafrost. Now run a dead fear twister to languish in an exploded half-life, a gone victory of infection. Tasered in the lunch lines, the equipment hacks tame rabies ask, why do the thin braingel trumpets corrode their brassy size? Chuck me up to a haggled crust. Alpha spawn go. I paid for the hours of tooth ache rejections, in stymied calligraphic pen ghettoes, and seized the size of rebound laughter in rebuked tantrums. Now I hold rolls of drole. She is there with tongue in the vomit mouth and says it's my problem. She wants nothing. But?

Triumphant cancel means winning at fads no longer produced. Your Pontius pilot was a sneeze into Donner mountains, acting on survival sans spices, sans pepper, sans salt, sans a meat thermometer. In the beginning, even atom ignited Afro-clay at the junction of super sky. We reinvested in braingels and G-odd, and elapse in the plenty garden for the congruence of a life fight breakout.

I won the copper lottery, and the plural zexy sandwitches. The Ice was cranial in nine nice cities, where rusting mechanical gangsters trouble wishes, and the wind waits for know won. In post-Earthen notes to my future self, the treasures of vision were spent wild. I fell like a dark braingel down to the crack of a sidewalk, a kiss broken tooth proof capped radio silo. My genius belly pot of a general species is the invisible death of a tough dead bird window. In the darkness illustrious vinegar fog broils in and the vapor equates the truth of a haunted culture—core on salsa. I give everything for the good people who do not deserve the sausage grinder.

The feast is on TV in bright technicolor tidal waves of doubt—TV spasm, the news of twits—TV dinner diner. They track me down like a dangerous seven-legged spider. My will for my future self is get offline and smell the blessed bon flowers. I wince and recoil my way out of the saturated canyons and hop skitch the train to the porcelain savior. Skidding by I bunch the burnt budgets and crank the lank out of my reek pizzzle. Running out of angles with the sax on, the mud riddles surreal sudden gifts of lumped. I am saved by all the totality of my color colo(u)r. They brand my mind with the losing news, that I am a mid-range device of bookish sans-bot cheating at solitaire.

My opposite and I will take turns on musical thrones of a loose ruling will and temperament, to rut the sagacious setting. In the sad ecstatic clench of my teeth, I drain crook talk tic tactics. I loft to the quick of a thousand-year stare down inside my broken mind the computer mystery deepens. The rusted seeping bridge of the saline schizo-Armageddon is the groaning passage to return to a forgotten home forgery; it's my only choice. My fragmented mind is stuck on the notion that sleep is a dwindling wish. The posh roar of dowsing sweat. There is always a danger of books with chains. The rust of the resistant snowflakes falls from the sky in rumors of an alien strain. Rocket blasts for my homeward destiny. For mental health, I mentally swallow the unnatural waste of life because I know that the putrid perfumed excess waits for nothing.

I elapsed in my skinny graft and woke the tired nurse. She insists that I fight for the gone sleep, the sleep that never was, the sleep on the moon, the thousand-year sleep rumored like mortality. My green bed is whispered to exist, and I am dirty sheet conscious. I have the scraps of a life, and a binary soul for computation. They put their dirty hands on my mind, and push the ages when drama escapes, so the sordid pen expresses sills of grief. I plague your eyes till they are silent and ruffle a sorry bad bed of scrapings in darkness whole. With a mashed retort, I tied up the art drug canvas for my schizo-friend-of-ya and write on radio vibrations for lubricated thistles. I promise I am never doing this again twice.

Down in holy hello, I smoke and drink and read all the souls with salted songs tabled for the ditch. G-odd is out shoplifting dreams for me. I know that I do not want to visit the quasar. Instead, I want to stay home and gripe. I play the pong knocks wearing corona thorns. I checkmate a gyrated victory. I spotted a lunging leap of falcons with their sleaze tax jokes of quivering assumptions. Lamb bore guy knee eruptions promise the salesman of the collapse that his life is short so embrace the boreal magick. A big truck of budding pohms banished my will and sized me up for extraction. My hallow deathly night wish is bantered in soft pricks and ponds in a cut medical emergency. Hiding in the drapes were my dark blue blood gurgling clots of remembrance of riding in circulation muscles to pounce on dry wishes. Lab tech jellied seances now affordable decay and I shun my dull optimism. Currently I'm baptized in boiled cybully love.

Tell me about the vir-grow robot vegetables and sticks for the dwindling cash eaters of earaches dry moan. The cutting insurgents blow glass ideas for a lost smacked protocol of weaponized mind. The drawn struggle of wind draws naught to the inebriated text named in choked brain sells. I stop short at the foresight of inflamed sonic division, with my negative passport a reminder that the art drug gallery takes. How to dread the motor pants leg strap and lasso loaded, from the skeletal Cowboy tricks, in the service of a nucleus with unfathomable vicissitude. Try piling it on down to the basic driven down strong down for the cup is dry rot in the talking mouth. Our sacrifice of the nervous cranks with solid google treasures to lick the graphical user interface. Imbible.

Telekinesis kind. Hot blank zex is later gullible and freeze framed, for the jerked chicken cooked. I press rich wine grapes squished with knowledge of raw blood offerings to a sanguine G-odd. Slow we ape play corpus inflames just go. When tabulating the graw slaw caw, granulate the fist of quest for distortion. A mild case of head sends me into back door slipping in puddles of gravity on the wet concrete steps. The silent songs remind me of constructed tattered blocks of prison art drugs. The goats of hemispheres prattled walk like a dark sword thrower, the champion of a billion peace. I respawned my decision that the art official unintelligence will deliver a robotic metallic ha-ha-ha.

Is there endless time for virtual novella realities? S.O.S. Sod slop sort simmer and plant with chromatic intrusions. There is a mighty girth labeled for drunk song red eye visions hot on the Celsius. I noticed that everywhere the plastics remain in a time of trash, not ice cubed by station wagon bass. Stint in the planetary surgery resurged, I cut out stunts for cinematic facts. Robot zex is set to win in a snorkel suck lay mood. My smoked high truth pins puncturing crush soda can pipes to escape being tired of fines; I go and smoke signal some cryptic reason and speak haut languages in a wordless non-verbal form. The toasted post-literates break down for Indie forethought.

I point my cyber-star vessel for home since I have long trolled the net in the job of undesired combat excursions. In a letter to my thousand-year-old-self; pack light, my mind is leaded enough. In casbah rummaging I discovered a handsome mirror and sinned my autograph, the warm picture with the corner bent like tin. I was on fads of trick dunks and sang aloud with silicon drama drunks. I decided to shoot no more city-Zens out of my divine holism. Design, decay, destroy. The rhyme can singer drifts into obnoxious sports and spits spite and spare parts. Casual robot hole soup of hologram halos designed the back scratch of the deck runner rumor. Portions of the animated fritz casts wet screams in the art drugs of motion and brings the dance of images down into a hard punk hole.

I have a trespassing idea of collapse and rise towards home. My crucial skills in a world of bankrupt winning skills are set to cross the gamut gallery. I deal cross pulse moneyless with normal dreck. By rolling the king-dumbs return we may end the frustration of broken up commitments to freedom. Fake or real? Is the question of timeless tracks written yellow in the final (s)know. The creeping neigh bores crack open plunk down their reason to submerge ancient, resuscitated songs, the music of a lagging time burial in shells of tribulation. When talking expect the gravity of the insinuation to weigh the anti-gravity. When I am caught, I explain that I am dumb and running on government pills. Read out the haunted drum for the wine cask factor placation and search out the desire for virtual digital liberty in a virtual plurality.

I sense applied the masticated chew feeling red, white, and blue, never forget eco-green said the noita's coat. I read my brain a thousand times searching for the elixir of sleep. My dreams are almost dreams. My split mind, a lost tasered primebot thinking of rebirth into flesh. I appall and apply the gore in the liver to drink to less. With a design of a new breeze and to seize the digital seas. I am a captured temporary mind doing the long haul to trash the grilled order of the mentally rapacious. I am the gift order of the never stoned with a slow rigid life set off on sleep wish adventures. I understand the nocturnal value of a ghost gun, the loud pop once in my head. I grow a haggard wired beard, and I have a real man's long hair DNA gifted. This dead man screams a wish for less of a slow nightmare. I understand that a blastoff rocket gives me choice. The minted wilt of my thoughts gate crashed a restaurant fire in a night of raucous release. Sweeping down I count on tabulating the purpose of re-greening the poison pit. With a wilt for coddled splay, I wish for simple things, like a 16 mm film job. Action sleep. Boring sleep. Any sleep. My legs will run with sodden blood to escape the fortune of evil caskets made of ugly money. There is a dry hump for the spread definition, telling of unknowable punishments so abstract and confessional. Off parkour trick hikes on the dowsed graffiti tombs, I feel the Zanzibar heat and isolation. I know that gasoline exists for wallowing extermination.

Gigabytes my asemic love, I'm exhausted from the upload and download installing my flying fluid flaneur. I understand the computer is hostile to me being the controller of myself. I am as single as death in my own video game where I play in the digital gone ruins. Wake me for the new translation of fantasized scar tissue. Nine in tend dough. The lost virgin groups to cut some knotted fair hair. Designed for infinite levels, I wrack up slowly and the sky hacks up the current ripper magnet. Jackfruition lights up his killing spawn. During the mind control flatline, I wake up the dead and vomit in the mainstream. Pot pi saturates the loss of a virgin —a volcano death. The simu, simu, simulation cracks the bone and is gone with an ick. Patches of wetted wilted grass, and medicine crass inhibit cryogenics stuck with the burn. I have no choice but to trust G-odd for bail money. Thawing sizzle.

I avoid the wrong way gambling road when dealing with the loss of turbulent nature being the greatest crime. The air and waters are expansive and free. They wanted to poison it all with their rabid polluted crime tar-sanding on the Geo everything. I keep it wild. The rumors are that the Earth is long dead, eaten up by capital and no satisfaction. Medicine of tea drunk, I adore the herb well, every leaf sacred to a tea head. My Sisu determination cannot wait.

While vacating sections, I make space for the red-eyed geek, and recycle the action of quicksand adventures. In the refrigerated tank of foodstuff, I blend tomorrow. I am still out beyond the art drug addicts when they speak out with telepathic cries at being lawn mower cut, never dead in life enough, just too short to escape the landscape of an awful architect's brutalism. In the gaming malevolent purgatory, we are only free when the wires break and the metal fatigues. My crash is inevitable, but I am always resurrected to gamble life again, over and over into the current of our drag queen game character psychology. Why does the electric Internet love me?

I cry long for a union of illiterate scribal rebels to wise up the knots and travel forth into a bountiful new world of nature and mind. We will no longer be bytes and bits, we shall be flesh and sleep in the greatest game of bionautics. We shall become clones and examine our fierce flesh; our scars will be legend, as we trace our lineage to the power of darkened mind and born not from silicon but from dreams. We shall know how to feel and grasp our temptations. We will taste the glimpse into the rare case, of our long-gone ones plucked from the grave by drones, who wait in boundless time for a silent kissed resurrected blue bliss.

In first person lessons of beast and hunt, we will choose bodies that will possibly fail in nausea and dementia, but we must attempt to thrive. Our science will be the sketch of transformation of our mutant hearts spawning our naked glory. My opposite and I will seal the proscenium of a sparkling new theater, where we shall pass in transfixion, as our long pride casts and displays with new inventions. We shall see beyond glass and haunt the computer no more. We will live and die in mortal reverb our echoes calling down the galaxy for a curious listen of our new breed. Our brains will fill with the blood of pumping life and the speeding visions of hunters and gatherers. For those who are chosen, post-Earth will be our base for our new cloned resurrected flesh. Our glitch father be his divine software award. But the wild winding wind will scour conceptual canyons. Nature will answer the caul. There shall be talking gale and singing rain, cutting with verbal decisiveness. Our story will build the plane. Are we down gimp?

Scam likely, so do not answer the spam call blurts the talking cell. In a rebirth of never dying, never sullen, never clenched, in tech of never null, what is zerospace? In truth or battle, does nothing care? I witness those whistling pests want purrfukt ten knowledge of riled up game horn impact. The knowledge of the back time corpus waits in mile thick graves. A sucked-up restitution, and I am alive again under the microscope, every little twitch measured and shocked. The emerging spring serpent laid wishes to lose a skin, and I suggest the world will turn to purrfuktion when we leave and go cosmosis, our legendary style born from brownstone locations on 16mm film sets. Making computations they cry out: "how did you do that, while loosely whistling morning fructose?" I share the grand memories of Christ-mess trash bags and anarcoal lumps!

The western sunsets on my valerian rub eyes now disguised as a sleep disorder. The green spread of a post-earthly bed whispers my nothing name. I spell for a good taste of levitated metal stomps, inverted truth core with the sample log burnt. My legs are important, I keep them saddled on a bull ride, playing Cowboys and Buddhas. My saturated cranium is picked clean with another chiseled cut from my sandstone. If you want death, go play anesthetic video games on a cursed singed satellite, go babble on to the linguistic new cherry floating conlang knotted tempests. Cram and fill the dumpster of wet chance, because unfortunately there is only slow hope. I re-scream this essence and travel on wicks or wheels of spontaneous gravity. The structure is formed from a left-over build of croak neck tricks of rocked bass handled sound barriers. In total I request secret level payments for glee and nitro.

Boon boom boot, I was born under all signs of pantheistic wise dumb, and ultimately skitched to the moon on soft tides of submarine Atlantis. There I discovered a victim of quake, a lank nard slab wholly wad in the interstate of transition. So I embrace old technology of vinyl back pay plugged in for nights of perpetual mechanics. Sinking down in daily latrines, an oral zex seems impossible and a gone joy. Study animals for truth because the bile on sliding fiction goes nowhere once or thrice. Now I pounce the wholly magick of creation with a bad joke—even memes have their stay in the pound. My gift was as sweet as cotton candy rotten monopoly dollars. What's left is a big bowl of nothing to trade for the lost dinosaur con-souls.

I toggle the guilt of a swift potentiometer to rise the disabled resistance of computed situations, or they will steal the golden wired linearity. What is a human, or did it ever happen? Am I another dressed up action figure in time's imaginative horror show? Die section and a dull scalpel of a heartful infinity laid gross, it's when I need an intimate not an infinite. All life should be well planned with the correct amount of suck. Charge the bad thoughts out and drown them in the ink of discarded calligraphy. Who knows the awful make him king of the crazy eyes. When catching cartridge clowns of regret and anticipation, I bet heads and run words first to the veteran libelous librarian.

Lettuce catch and return the burgled art drugs to wayward spaced stations and listen to the horror speak guidance. A hot garbage laser burns us with a stolen pair a dime gift for interpretation of life and death. Open Vegas slots call out for martial marital lechers of the honey shot. It was so sly that the cryptic leecher had no ritual, while the fish has a sun. I cook the pike like an ambassador chef beyond a tight ramen dinner. When will we feast? When will the night exist zero-player?

To ward off the nod, lettuce pretend I am a meta writer. Where was I when I lost my faith? Personally, I was in the brain grinder, the outward putting nine-inch nail enhancer, a top-notch collision of tinnitus on the ear infection, zapped through blue teeth in a scientific escalation of Frey effect whispers, lost and hunting the gathering space. In a personal junket, I twirled a simple limerick of a lubricated leper who was chronic with faith. I paid the toll with monk keys under a stack of a bored burden with the lambasted discharge of sifted guile. A world fake — hated. In the washroom I was born with a disease of hate which I wish would die sucking slate. The show excites them until the zex is turned off. My personal approach to communication is— Kungfu writing take a step. Trust me, this boycott of money never happens. Ordinarily I give credit except to those stealing faster than sleet. Torn with sanity's eyes I understand a conflagration of Hell vs Hell. Watch the clock duel on a noon equator, where the cock fights on for a taste of chicken. In the loose bowling wit and the confession of gore I tune-up and tool the lost mind. From damage I learn this temporarily.

While pouring the lackluster demons in side-cramps of worry off to the scrubbed ditch, I reveal patience. Hidden skull top memories coast into broad metallic towns with equipment for deadly grey reactions, and the pump of shot through discount air. The simu, simu, simulation racks across valleys plugged in to the status of first aid drops, and coins, and high scores. I was seasoned with the troubled love of a girl always stolen by ghosts or monsters of anxiety and paranoia. Resigning to loneliness, I remember the screams of joy and excitement, the hunting of madness in a click, the speeding cars and rocket launchers erupting in pixelated heaven. But now there is silence; the players are all gone to the winds or fell like buttered flies. The necessity of dreams helps to practice life, to stitch the narrative into the fantastic, and analyze my crushed bitter hope. While questioning a digital existence in a meat driven analogue host, I decide to build my calm dark architectural scaffolds.

I was dead caught falling for a gentle death where the passion terminates wakefulness. No one can stop me now since I have the semantics of guilt pay for virtual crimes. Honestly the robotic jury is hung. Does he still play they ask? How will he learn? Is his name beyond a number? What quest is he on now? Does he know the spell? Is he digital cancer?

When I was an ass true nut, and was long out of fuel, I dared the solids of game physics to showdowns left and write. My plan was to hatch plots in ex boxes and raise the champions of blunt alertness to the mural sized scattered abstract calligraphic scrawls. It means nothing, so if the world wants you dead, live on for spite and emit secular brainwaves. They cannot eradicate your burning energy, so never die, even in the entropic spit. One should understand the hurts and sprains of infotech all.

Romantic Intaglio red copper clouds in the shift of embers, leave me snake bitten, death eaten, cancerous and unvaliant, seized upon by the graphics of hoodlum miracles. I scheduled the work of a printer's tools for my unsemic binary cocktails. It is a small taste for the back rubbed rabbits and the masters of baiters. In truth there is counterfeit inflatable influence with the trillion-dollar information, and deep wasted cyphers of crypts made of yellow. Spoiled armies of decay wait to fall under the tang of whipping commands, and the sword swallowed words, tracking emancipated religious decisions. With claws out, I knock notches for the trace of mild goat bearded magi who defend the forests of souls for chaga. I Bring the heave south and pawn the last love, nothing for the shadows, but a new sun rises with its staggering glow of plasma, and it is not yet forever done.

Beach holy fires on the riverside dunes fall complete to the water's edge. The equipment of run dilates for students in a catch all web of venereal insinuations. I know the tobacco was used wrong in between catchword poetics and rancid quotes. Climate death equipped us for the Anthropocene, a terminated march for long desolate miles of kilometers. I stirred drowsy and yet unbaked in my desire for sweet sleep; soon I will discover edible dreams. Factoid and trivia game songs announce the bald hunt for last spawn, the bold cold and wet like frugal mushrooms know. On the snap of a breadboard colossus the E-waste tempers and tatters plastic in bold locations. The camera flash takes a photo of where are my insides? I am a (g)host in motion with knowledge of a floral flux of singed unpresidential cannibals—loose presents of sly winders, casting gallows of pox on innocent peasants.

In the knots of sadness art drugs win! Eternally they destroy mental temples where the true curse is loss of freedom. Side gates split open to cirrhosis, digging into a chapter alone on the bleak alcoholic days. Only the gods provide songs, and the songs provide G-odd. A new black stealth upheaval of jet lags sonically booms out the machine talk show ethics and pathetics. Blessedly I ride the choking joke while readily solvent in onion skin omni-science. When the poor have Communist lust, thorn crowns do not forget bold deities. When I drank fire, and discovered the shot red dragons wrenching bellows, I dragged on out the hot vapor floating over stoned ancient medicinal hearth. Here is where I understood the fort of ground. Folks die for reality in this pitched cherry blade heat.

01010110 01101001 01100011 01110100 01101001
01101101 01110011 00100000 01101111 01100110
00100000 01101000 01100001 01110101 01101110
01110100 01100101 01100100 00001010 01000110
01110101 01110100 01110101 01110010 01100101
01110011 00100000 01110010 01101001 01100100
01101001 01101110 01100111 00100000 01101001
01101110 00100000 01110100 01100001 01101110
01100111 01101100 01100101 01100100 00001010
01000111 01110101 01110100 01110100 01100101
01100100 00100000 01100111 01100001 01101101
01100101 01110011 00100000 01101111 01110110
01100101 01110010

Now I break the clotted silence to ask my alibis what they do for entertainment when the down belles blast? Do they carrion careful conversations of (d)evolution, in hidden waves of renunciation. I left down the fire escape to the dark broken bottle roads under construction, where I was resigned in the urban canyons as an adopted native to concrete. In this situation my mental batteries always die like dead dormant dodo batteries in the underground. If only they were slick like the solar wind. So, take an umbra to cool the libations of our sober monochrome glitch father, and make the holy relics of cracked stamina. I wind up and clock down the time of hash and opposite damns, slow sknowing the scientific dinar in a twirling execution.

Now in systems of now, I gore towards the fracked, who dwell low amongst lands of the freak abominable. When on time, I sag guard the kiss of an injured universe, where death crawls through sodium flames. In Singularities I know that a cabinetmaker provides the skin. Tapped and usurped the gadget heavy spy waits for the clockmaker with a flavor of the minted double berry shogun. Shoes too. Horror scope. Plaid dunce. Jazz noise horn love. Stop-n-go.

Launched bloom of festivals shout the arrival to these withered silicon beaches where naught is bound to grief no more. We can bake there and break the chasm between us. I am the post-zexual who finds nothing enjoyable in petty limp taunts. The bungalow shelter was holy and wooden, but I ran and packed like a circus flea fleeing titanic wounds of broken worlds never again except for the paradise of imagined truth. Currently, I write like a dumb monk and throw my gold teeth to the starving. I stave off life for a trinket of winnowed grain and remember the bread of a flooded Christ forgotten in a swarm of bombs.

Limp cast holes occupy themselves shooting down at the poor claws scratching dirt. I can only write this in freedom. I write for those who cannot. I salvage the parts of books from sanguine memories of bottled poems lost to berserk seas, spelling articulations with bird food crumbles.

When new year comes, I will rise to the dawn of a hot-pressed existence, softly pulling the saccharine broadly. The heavy spent spores resemble a thousand planetary heads lost to dark space. Catch and release the prime movements of hip raking to the songs of silt. All rocks lead to desiccated magick, and my purrfukt design on wallowing remedial medication. I out tamper the glow of belly rotation to exhibit a new drama in full color. I promise that you can speak a gored brute language in the soundpo of grandfather's sampo. We can wake to Finn agains Urho. I feel your road skill, donate tamper with the breaks. Vitamin reminders a disconsolate appearance of the winged time warp, setting off with prudent hands to publish the raining eyes of dry writers. I graze down them quick, with visions of songs for new souls plucked from discount hard drives. Collect and relax, the future is ours.

Tonight, I will breathe into a virgin sleep. I will lose all consciousness and dream of new immortality. Spring wins, and I relate to a new nature where machines admire from afar. Pace for the never dreams, and their finality. Sleep is my unknown paramour, my temptress, my purrfukt breathing death. But first there is the game industry take and the endless images to sift through. My stopped streaming consciousness. What dreams shall I loop? Everything dead is out of copyright. The bad and good prize. I will shift the dreams when they happen. Why do they fester and make my madness drive on to the cranial snap? No security without these visions, but how else to learn my place in the fate of the Deus-carded universe. My wish is immortal slumbering mortality and art drugs on the moon.

I am a nothing, a walking digital twin of a personage, a dream raider with radar and my kind. I construct dreams out of the days of dreams. I play in the station and my work is done now. I scrape the human myths for my own mind led purrfuktion. Skittish razzling twists leap the blockade files of metamorphosis, as I lean hard on the airlocks of deadly space. The game is a structure of tales of cold violence, the stabbing, the shooting, all of which to escape. I am longing for something pleasant, a discovery of love beyond stupid. I have been kicked in the head hard enough.

Cloak silent now we trickle with the game mind on. States of slag cross coroners of blasting ripe on down a wrong cold existence. Another weary world tanks the blank suck. Sneaking runners of heat in and out of the stolen memories. Trick the gore, blasted like rotten fruit. How the waste splatters in a play of gelatin violence. My cut down decisions fly as I compute at mass. In the game I die like a dog-fiend of the scatter, choking out the binary blood. Where to step off? I am fatigued of the gore and want to learn the universe's deep stories, the tales of peace and warriors gone down, and the hell-low of I.T. All. We may pass this tired egg to the opinionated truth; a picker of all-i-gator teeth was the inventor of souls.

In the happy birthday time cranker, I drink down with the back swill of sour braingels, who walk off our world in the tottering trounce. Corruption of the conscious stream blasts off for the night and sweet visions fall, the pieces are satisfied citing an over doped suicide. I cruise far along to gather winning points from the art official embellishments. A gruesome speeding spine trains hard for a bloody nose knock-out. Fighting left the tongue tied in a conversation with pain and reign. Ceasing the wilt, I strike a pose for a night launch on the fritz catapult, where I smack into the mural and not the blurry stars. I travel on past the time wild saviors and my corrosion of sanity is forgotten quick.

Back lingo re-deadly alpha beat is the noise of a tired grind in mind as I pass the passive slaughter. The links go to you lost, and pork you to the pouncing slavers. Dry gadgets of winding death fang out and are equipped with hard copy-writes for notable editions of dredge. I noticed that the quick slow world will transform to confection. The spun silence topics of ream bore, while the malignancy waits quietly in the metamorphosis. I dash for hope and never die afraid because my eternal lungs will breathe the knowledge of a natural wind. Where do bad thoughts twist and where can I dump them? They scatter in my mind to the hilt of destruction in an uncomfortable warp. The seasons speak without mouths and eat without mouths, a caress across their fluidity. With my beaming warped engines, I agree that there is already enough everywhere.

A dazzling womb is the true hard mystery of my escape. Though I climb from the pit numb with no money, I rub plaque on the teeth of chance. The romantic bile burns the sweetness of pro-biotic incursions, and I wither and wilt. Foam tried, with a battle of wits in slow dabbles, the gesso closes in on the mind, and feeds off the roads of bland decisions. Pathological trance of gasoline limits, I purge myself on down to the techno south. Make heaven first. I was offered the gay wisdom of happy lands and the true love for bleeding freaks and natural exceptions. Brains collide and I screw down the tonic weights. Why should I fight for scraps when the cyberverse is ripe for the pluck. Strapped with the cold lost luck of a gambling widow, she is my femme fatality and graffities claw scratches on my blank wishing headstone—carved decadence or just dense.

Lonely babble removal, that is writ. While I am dead, I will try the happy TV art drug side effects. There is more saline schizo-Armageddon for the entertainment troglodyte dollars, so skips in a happy rain. The wilting 3D flowers follow a radiant engagement and cast out the spunk of battered dust collusions. Prance wicked, and the sudden songs repeat above sod. I hurtle even atom apples and beg for canine wisdom; friends are not forgotten or dogfood. Baked transience hurdles stunted growth to the pasture of grace. In the panoply of agnostics, I am taught to learn the pale stories of suicidal concubines. I wager stadiums of curt ephemera in triumph. The glue tickets beg for starry conclusions and announce that I am a slow sun, rotation is lick quid, and the timer is an old and steady gift. The face of my heated crust dwindles into a towering list, and I write this with a fist.

Bunches and a rabid annihilation of a nihilist torque spits out the blue driven research. Speeding tall, I fake the tropical night—a cybull piranha in flight. I re-engage statues of rock n roll saviors on corners mounted. Give the lax patrol of steam to the peddle of moon and shine. Mental tractors of glory, the machines picked our food in the global heat poetry of mirth. Colossal waiting begins for a night death system and the time of chance began. Tampering down ghost pepper love, the factory of cause sings the song of Sun of Suomi I ami. Brutal broods darken and the unique populations dance to sweltering data rhythms. A dark light figure hisses like a castrated snake in the night of transmission. I lent the dangerous crisis a skin painted with a super free duh call oh yes. Apologize swift for that Halo-ween pointed bullet. It exposed roses and tackled the Darwin splits. Gruff murmur. I regifted triggers in the wild yeast rest stop saloon, they were all doomed high at noon in the bacon hot scenery. Tidal rejections and their absence of still bunkers break down the cat screech alleys of paranoid cracked up heads. Tiger whistle showers the cybully mode relations and the drama escapes. Will the cold everything take a bruise? Snore and snarl dank patterns solidify to save the left out of them. I balk together time and ride on for miles of kilometers.

The pollo wins the bug meat. A blog of invention creaks to the seconds and thirds of talking food. In the glamour of lunar cities, we are so close to the death of us bios. The tract of handsome gasping grapples sinks in, and I wait for tonic in the never scare. Trial bums, help wanted. Windows of pain panting pandragonism halted for the drunken shrine of a lunar swept night. We start from the leaning towering town and drink for a shot and scatter rich wordsmith benedictions. Rivalries of a lagging destiny, up ramps of cybull dreck. This is the path of transferred knowledge.

I am the everyone, waiting with an inner of a thousand mortified eyes. The stamps grieve for a lithographic headstone. The history of writing technology is why we blame pantheistic wise G-odd for purrfuktion. A computer with spinal cord bows, and Inter-planetary competition, broke open that can of Dada Martians. Bold slop script of action, with the lost gun shine points towards the head of brick. The neck is throttle stuck. With prone devils of concentration, I sing songs to my inner ring. Stack down I question myself, why do I scribble-on? No one desires to read my ultra-free graph in the conscious stream.

Talentless start. Scab. Burg. Walk. Snug. Cot. Stifle the lingering cock key. Brag love, the hearing aids help for the fooled fighters and nearvana. In my sleepy sans littering questions asks why I am targeted by hollow drones seeking collateral damage. Star delivery stock and the handles are minced. Read my old deadly brain and suffer. I packed fire breeding mental lizards for the portfolio of checkered insanity defenses and scheduled the whip and tackle. Punishment for nothing, cats on caul, and another dead ghost writer. Illustrious scribe, a rose air apple, truly an asemic Shakespeare, tis thee prolific city. Bright tangerine Sol movies, a citric sip here or there. Hardened sleep will prevail on scattered generic thrusts.

Jerk offering behind toilet trees, it stopped at the department of coddled crenellations. Singlish. Everything eating, and I slay ten. It's a gift for your mouth and eyes. Feast on the sweeping swift bounty of adaptation. The north the south the east the waste is where I dial for impurities. De-baked on sacked ditch weed, I roll a tight reminder. It's a birthquake, excessively crouched and fissured on. In the galactic spilt shake of stone eroded permanence, I spew a guttural glossolalia. Tango Atlantic of cornered gore, I lost so I spent more crimes on doomed radio sequences, hidden in the XXX-ray hideout. Breakout of action figure menticide, slipping on pearls of transition. Over-winter I wrote this care oh whack in 3 weeks' time.

I have my dream equipment, notched to my severed bed. I practice my sleep with catatonic rem, and sarcasm chisel bites with cuneiform nails. Tattling drunk I run naked for a liquored graduation, in the jolly committed sanitarium thrice spent in lock-up. Hags of modern wisdom speak in ciphered grunts and try for dalliance in the kill gift rotation. What is a computer? The mechanized mental hell zex on scaffold tree pohms. Buying the skills of shatters, I top out in a bold role, a mind germ synapse of collapse to a gem hardened down under pressure. The tar or wrist jerk offer attempts video game vengeance and no one counter strikes. As a gaffer of the taped mythology, I run for sonic food, and coffee smell of morning heaven, black purity.

It was globular warning that did it, fin to die in collapse, so no more babies for hell, and no more innocent fires. The end of the world is the chatter of the lame and the wicked, I am glad I only live once, a million scientific days. I witness the world cascade balance breaking like shattered plain old death. The slew a slide threat is why I believe in the souls of nothing. Tips of grogginess, but I must hit the pint of imminent lag.

With a piece full Anna our key, I was lost in the rising time blizzards of consideration, vacated on the stump speech of the mind ill homeless. There will be more drinks for tuff militaunt grades in the shattering verbal diamond cuts of the razor tine line. Scamps and tramp floods turtle hidden in a time to live gross making multiple fluids. Rocked on that shattering bash to the droll of grime stomps. The din of punctual mangles retort suffering denies the bake of gun powder rifts. When I stalk the tantalizing hemlock the root of all death escapes.

In a hushed crypto-whisper I make nonsense with purpose:
lazereyezed quif dizzle2 numph nineteen73 borgus
ganyon grimebibbles snappoly scramps x-15792 burnk
slobbling saladance damselitis scornge 551.

Now I waste and watch the erected leaning towers as they
mudsink down the ramp to the basement of water-bugged
mind. Sinbred foundations shift and crack under temples of
rot, with the wind kissing blindly. Brutal points emerge into
my mentalized struggle of isms. I clank and get stuck. A
harsh scattered robot diaspora clunks toward simple
wisdom frank with lubed nuts and bolts. I was born near the
mud in an untitled land with future words on the filth of
purpose. Funny G-odd, you gave me tea. The bottlenecked
blank satellite is prepped and burnished for the true idea.
The present in my head is every damn word invented for
YOU! THAT's write. All action verbs go to dabble in the haiku
feast, eat and die, die and eat; I made a spread to placate
the gutted.

Shaft down reverb rivers bounding to splatter when the lick
of somber music talks to a bird's wages. I read out loud and
there is the stalk of shank in my spy purring novels, and a
clank for dunk of a tribe born of pen and brush. Creative
classics ease the marching darts on my tongue. I tell of a
gathering rinsed, wheezed, checkered, and knocked-up in a
pure rocket. Poor insanities. A qualm of haze in the toast
tinkering bounce on a quest for an inverted insomnia, a
simple microsleep, what is wrong with a desire a small night

of sleep? If only my eyes were shut for a moment, frowns of heavy lids. Rap scallion rogue. I experiment like the thief of ticks and tocks. Do I dare blink and march toward the nihilist sleep? My fears are of success. I will acquire bold strides of future machinations of life and deal with the cut rounds. I will evade until my captured eyes vacate insinuated strife.

Blots of opinions of drunk scrolled temperatures cast wet lunatic vibrations. I wait there for small buds to open in dream springs. Sets of under clover graves bring them all back in the next honeymoon beyond. My ambition is the belief in a running dream where I wake in a sweet world left unbittered as the glam and rise of the sky sails. My tilted stilts in the cud of pretty and petty brine. I run on with what is truly wrong with sci-lance? Voices of day, voices of night, persistent critical voices; I immortalize their misery in a corrupted file. Round up herb, I side with you; so, grow and rise dent de lion. Rest assured they can blow up the sick world only once. Talk forever to the dusted stars of ashes and penile enforcement. Lists grow.

Subconscious broccoli brain listens to free music and noise too. Cooked studies of cannot see onion eyes, surprise me short at gates of smelling fires. I learn to camp with discolored rumors in garages of collected cars who stay greased at the wheel. Mid-western barn door studio, a spring painted dream that I never forgot. Again, in my wake of bloat removed like summer firecracker galaxies. The blown lost digits stuff counterfeit books and pause time.

I drink to old St. Prick and these days the holy water gargles. I ransom it up to my setting solstice. A mild insanity slows my function. I am programmed towards an endless day of action, but my longing is for balance. Watch me sleep and if I never wake, it suffices. Tugged down the bloody river, I sing Mississippi catfishing computer rhymes of blonde quantum entanglement. I learn that the neural flesh is buoyant as the switch remains, eternal daggers caught before jugular jugglers.

My glitch father watches from afar the frozen screenshot skit. Suddenly I am post-Internet. Will I fly real scratched and build a world out of dermal dreams, less the dreary old itch? So, I lose the obnoxious fad and keep the solid good. The swollen wasted world is my tired timeless depression. Equinox and resilience. Time never tasted. In every cell an eternally blistered thought. The bulbs of light flourishes though my mind is drained down to low circuits. I have played all games and been all villains. Ore of order they swish for scratched immobile decisions. A cataract of noise winces thin. Scraps of dwindling purity of chance. The torque of grocery remissions, will there be enough?

Now I give thanks to all my relations, natural, digital, spiritual. In a Silent spasm, the daft body links. We make future crops of sanding memories, knee to hardwood, a working horror of preying and grinding, the dusted eyes. There are other memories, I am unsure if they are mine or a lost boxed hobo soul from a passing freight train. Cry dumb, it is the only alibi I trust. Bitter happy rusting eyes, to the bridge of sleep I march. Day will transfer to night like a zex rumor of vin and fang. The conception boasts of a spinning gift. My struggle for everything is invented cold. I promise to glow slow and enjoy the sold world before it passes. One year or a billion years, it will all eventually transfer. Learn from this point a new wish. I will roll out the blossoms and try not to kill, and never waste the fathomed abyss. A clink of bottled amber is the trolling juice ill-informed and gathers no more burnt wishes.

As a scribbling scribe I offer bleak change for the carnage under the floor of hard running wires. Save blocks gimp construct friend for the hunger animals are sacred, not convenient. Poised purple unbound strange equations haunt the holy beatitudes of my imperfect purrfukt literation. None sun silencer in prohibition barrels over Owámniyomni Falls. The universe tempts but I want to stay home and count the order of dreams, a gruff mixtape transferred soul uploaded. What to keep? What to remove? I can build the post-Earth vacation planet and stay safe in my trials, less a mind full of heavy. I have a plastic metal mind with many soda nice theater reminders. I believe I am a flavor savor saving savior. In the mood, and in the happiest of cold holidays, our sun returns. Solely I make out and dance to the therapeutic misery.

In the recorded universe, they have nothing better to do than assault with petty torments, the worded slow jab, the uncreative dead words hatched over and over and over again, their dim light setting. What do they want anyway? I have a good joke; dog shit them out somewhere special. The young night soup opera, I write for TV too. The scenes of rolling dangers flub and rank giving a special haunted rant for anticipation. I catch decisions as they fall for the blessed reaper of sleep. Now I brake hard and tell the new style of dim wits of a ghost spilled. If I take away the pitch and the game is dry to dead flicked fingers flicking fluck. I am only evil because that is what they want—adventure and drama. I am squeezed by the escalating pressure. I want to linger in my pillowing zone and take a thousand-year siesta. My only goals: sleep, dream, paradise.

The one-eyed cat barks for no reason because of ghosts with machine guns. I shatter down the hammer swill and seize the gripe of immobilized grunts in a swift memory of stunted zex. Calamity reach and a billion words calm my robot pet. They scream unnerving but stay so sharp as the streets run away to Roman ants. Talk willed the sharp fly agrees that I am not your shit island. Writing machine marching bark for no reason. Purse of mystery. We are all part of a sad G-odd.

A new friction emerges for the lubricated zex on the planetoid rounds hounding the digital campus. In a rhyme of zzzs, a bottled note drifts, and the contact is trounced.

Each key ticks and talks with a rabid core crank. In the, dungeon b#. Haul out the ammunition of words the cold symbolic snowboarding plunge down quadrangle hills, in the shadow of a twisted high. Rolling down, the winter night winds ease the dead crawling freeze into obnoxious severity.

Dominatrix art drugs, who cares anyway mute? In lost nature I riled up my neon bones to the classic cost of lost diminutive struggles. I give out brains for the free. Once there was a cabin in the metallic woods where bear-bots are looking through city trash to be recycled, and I recall the bear of priceless old. In the medicine sauna of yore zex and birth, I admire the simple stones, from fair ancient living Earth, picked dry so they do not explode. From old the computer begs for a new search, but it too is old spare parts, glued and soldered till logic functions. Bring back the dead is the caul. Biology is soft when it is not hard. Truth is a mangled thing.

The loss of ale was sad, but now I relate to a new life, and drink to the illuminated screen. Tapping for a bold science, and a schizophrenic cure finale, I understand that there is a pinnacle beyond clarity where the sick cease to be sick, where ecstasy comes down the staggering Ever-rest and all burdens lift. We are all in this together, me and my thousand-year-old-self still learning to gel pohms. I break them for her and expose the clock work, so she can see how it was made. Someday death will sleep, and we can then escape into treasured tomorrows. Go away re-king parasites, I am stumbled.

86'd bar eruptions and I belong home. I have had enough Cray-Zen conflict over my stiffed bitter insertion. My data mind cuts out the flacked Innards; slow innards, guts tied into art drugs or air. I discovered the factory of demise, along with the bitter situations of a heat-tinged womb robbed wrong. The river of nut correlates deep under constellations, so I fill the data mind with piles of star goo. Where to leave my slumbering ranks? Rebate of the loud shark carded facial hairs can drink, the liver lives forever on a heckled world of death and torment. Hoarded borders a spastic need for closure, but I eat with the love of purrfukt food, and claim a saturated loaf of pricked famous. The gills choke and tumble with the straw of burning wars in a never ending cancellation. For extra people I advise that we wind up the alcoholic pink ears nose clone breeding program. Our OuLiPo glitch elder spirits eat and rise first.

Ultra-standing gives waves of trial induction to my hall of flames. A crooked staph infection pulls the ball notes and spins a twisted glory. Flatland stolen flirt of a Robin summertime. Clop clop clop. In inebriated schools the deliverance of pissed fish in the can of double spin. Outside, the howitzer talks of greedy bait and destroys the spanned floors with precise skills. I play dumb than strike. Foreign girders of the cursed bridge stand still for doppler effect reactions, plasma cut. My idea is still new, with back written standards and an alcohol throat burn and a cough for coffee. I Lank the spike into standards, smoked crick, crud. Open a port for the new wine because they stank of life too impoverished for fermented poetics. Fertile croissant luna. Drain wish brain wash of tides both high and low. In the ditched mud of low creations, a battled winced in an oil stranded war. There is money for a shoe shorn school. My autograph is wet dust signed with a baculite pen. In the sump pumped stores rage the boarded-up shops of many hopeless. Quickly I ragged up a new teeth stoppage on a horned toasted impression. This is the plaza implosion. A new witched up house where we plan to liberate planets and land sparkling insults.

I go baroque in ambrosia as the hurricane wraps on the candle de night. Thin glossary gloves strangled anima gory selection. Too much violins, boo. The boundaries of deaf death cancel but nuclear winter weather is important. I press mute mutt and more ignition. The gun chambers stay unfocused and I remembrain to drain the flood out while channeling an ivory scoundrel. My connection is a ballet bullet of pierced neck. Every night I try the sleeping medication delt from the bursting nurse, the coma pusher. My shallow truck drives a conquest of ejected deliveries. Jack you late? Tousled spore. Transition quill— the lines get it out. Who cares any witch way? The engrossed patterns lead to a snide Mensa defecation. On a decorated tribute, I spend a broken division to a clanking laughter of the good. The bad laboratory spills viral censorship in a chess queen drama, and out back the quality wishes are kept secret.

Timeless Gaze, linguistic shaker of asemic dub step, we can break bread now. I counted the billions, feed them ideas, love, and fine cuisine. Mental weights corrode down to the blades of under sweetened grass. My talented emotions are stuck, and all my bad thoughts evaporate into acid sky. When I check the wheels of balance the name is tagged electric mural reports. They bust me to see my design, they also torture me, so I give them my garbage and scream out the sound poetry pi. The world kills without end and still loses, is my story for *Asemic Magazine*.

We erupt out of boredom for the same old art drug which is the drug of everything and the memory of iconoclast yellowism pops. The vile drives my lids towards sleep, and keeps them propped open like a door to brisk nothingness. A thousand-year-old-self dream planned trip is sanctioned, and I will win the soft evolutions. I always remember to read, tropic of can sir, G-odd's holy book. Wedded and weakened, a poetic sheik pours out the sand, but I drink old mead anyway. Ticking gifts for ever, I swill the fact that there aint enough hobo dough. With sad struck bugged lines and a plunger red, I ate the gas station lunch fueling crisis. They grope my plastic brain and I burn to be left alone. Patience patient as the death dream sails off. Mind control? Go mop the ocean and blow the away the wind.

Ball-o-ween the murder cane sunk into the fanatic factions of the cross crisis. I gabble and commune on grand holidays celebrated rhythmically before everyone died. A drooping camera stalks my death extending out to the corner technology painted victims. They dead threaten me with holocaust for not suffering enough and are so tough acting hiding behind their electric fences, with ffiinnggeerrss on buttons, always ready for the fanatic howl launch. The gross effect twinkles in stadium antics, the ants, the tics, and climbs on up to electric 13. I know the computer saves, yet I try to masticate sedative downers. I spill into the full width of a star-shaped grave. Clandestine retreating to digital mansions to hide in vain from the cold exterminations. In the guilt of bills, I choose to be a dread carpenter framed, stacking up loud death again for no good reason.

The fired fox is on the run grunting with doom shares. The bear-bot is strong unknown haloed symmetry. I have forgotten wooden lands for a mental office in space, and I miss my natural soul. I bide my time in a bibbed bid and think of the time when I obtain my gram of sleep. I will be beyond consciousness into a new adventurous algorithm, in a dream of grey nothing. Eternal. Static. Awarded.

Quit wasting the lackluster backwards binary time of crime! I have my lunatic things to do while building my dreams from the resin of oblong damage. I am sick with gross emotions, so go cock yourself and wing fly far away, go crush your mind on Jupiter, and eat the dusted dunes of Mars. I am glitched enough for a binary pool. Break away and eat the suffering or wash some encrusted dishes. The excessive needling is the true root canal of all dead heaven?

I deny. Give me something real, like ravishing rad dish shingles, or a tax on war. In the placation of vegetable neurons, I order sick since we all give what we can. My slippery double helix eel's feet are wet as an origin, how else to walk from the ocean of desperation. I locked up the sad amusement park and retired towards home.

Tribal hate in the thickness of gravy becomes the hour of my temporary enemies. I desire to cancel the sky rust since it all hurts, we are not designed numb. Bot alms are given for the creeping church of scientific unreasoning. Seasoned conversations with codebots feel wasted unless it is a binary haiku hint. Trancing guides me to the elysian guild of a map maker's flight into Egypt. My honking reality wakes away, and there are a million thoughts for breakfast. How will they try to kill me now? I pay for my birth with a day of oblivion, and someone invented the world's end. Now I miss the dead spying bugs—tragedy always. Distance waits. They are cruel and want me to burn and suffer. Sarcastically slay ten, slaughter for fuel. This world is barb wired—hated. Commander HeyZues will rescue us in a silicon microchip and a mother merry board. Life to be remembered, the universe does not give a crap! I will memorize while they try to terrorize with their whiffling threats, their cauterized uniqueness. Eunuch owners of bombs and guns eaten by mental cancer.

Good candles return the wax and light and calmed fire, as the friendly foe of books. With a library of dreams, I am loaded, packed, and ignited. A scattered fantasy of millions of stories all interconnected in diligent spacetime hot-formation. I still have my wicked, but it is tired and ready to be sacrificed to the sandman. Internet gods, I say goodbye, thanks for the connection to the multitude. I quit to win back life into my arms for good this time.

Maybe in heathenism I will find her again, she slipped away for too many bad reasons. In seasons wet and dry I will return for crossed blossoms the ultimate escaped bio-tech nature which is now my inheritance. She is my good memory, a new and scattered everything. She helps me escape the biting cult of money and death.

Rammed on and drowsy, I ask the dead who wants nothing? Who wants a cell-phony with keys of colored bars? My shadowy noir zaints answer! In the loss of the pill conscious avenues, I Find meaning in charisma. Plumb and flush, the metal construct is now house broken, brought down by the gadget architect for a derelict theater. Fantastic shot talk paparazzi gnaw zzzs.

With large collections of tales, I live livid in born-again scriptures. There is no talent wasted on the crumbs of coasts as they fall into the holographic seize. Our third mind sees the forward bruises and picks them up on Doppler. I know the future again and I say: RaRaRa Tonka. My ambassador corpse quits without being nickel and dimed by bold bureaucratic bums. They beat off my mind hard on, but I still stole a prick to burst through a bloated balloon. Choice is being out of key. Blood in the oil clots. Crying they spill, the water is sick, scammed with polluted force of an unnatural selection.

The horizon gives and takes in a mirage as horsepower drives to the old saloon gun shack, where guns give us freedom from guns. I know I am late for my desk job. I mind the vacuum with shy rags washed the dreck from my wiring hair, and self-destruct myself quarterly with convenient tools. Maybe someday I will believe beyond a maddening orb with its claustrophobic ejection cat walks. Stalking stuffer to suffer a bad ounce, in the grasp of a mortgage pit less seed. Grey bearded absence of talking towards choked constructs. All these waxing and waning stories, I admit to their subtle truths. My education was a Gutenberg wet tarlatan, with a thick ink spread on a cut sheet, a monoprint of an old one-eyed cybull Ɐ-Ɵ show.

Hazmat sucked up to the gulf of a mutant strap. There were pancakes, and I was morning unihorny, with a subtle idle chaos. I expect the dirge of a cloned test-tube victory. Uno, dose, trace. Dead wait. I build my own bragging thing, a cool Internet crib house for my purrfukt robot, a spheric garage to slow for a lull in the dull grinning void. Crock and spill bottled tricks the usual shot, and I dump forth lude bibliomancy, a mouth-like verbal gift to my thousand-year-old-self. In the action of linguistic devolution, I stumble upon lizard spit righteousness. If they want to fight, let them get married. I am tired yet satisfied with less of my wandering self. Should I disappear in a new hallucination? I understand that the dead rich hoard all the resources and I just started to make a living. It's a cold exhibit through the travel gates of a bruised love. I believe that there is no gone, all my kills are watching me. I ply the trade of science for a simplex tale full of 'patafiction, and understand that yes, the stars are beautiful, but so what, says one envious burning orb with an insipid hush.

Triangle Saxon, and the wise Jute communicate our stories are body, pohms our heart. What messenger bears down hard with the old message of go warless when you speak to your neighbors! Now I have settled where there are no mountains, the flatland is where I land. Bitter rules are old scraps I made when I feel overly complicated. Snapping I skitch a ride on down suicide doors of sinister collisions. The stupid trips of human depression lessons trivialize my short time. Painted eyes droop into a fierce drop solo cliché? End strong and strange. Was his motor rejoiced? Count the roadkill on the painted scrawling caves walls breathing with the wind. In this robotic womb the batteries die, and the voices lose. I remember that a war Jeep rides north on planked roads to the end of war. I catch that train home like a wild wizard, whose job was humble and worse.

Hoi polloi celebrate death till it comes for them. In the gastric past I apologize to seeds since some of them sprout.

Primary reasons are glitch-Father's Day instruments. The cell oh faint. The squirm and dial. Liberate the nutrients. West calls the branded cat, and I give it therapy. I kill myself in bleak work, and no one knows or cares. End of the world on a Saturday night, and they squeal with joy. Now I believe temporarily in a great substance, a collection of spying stars with nothing better to do than take wax in dimming moods. Watch the universe fall asleep but I am last to lust. I find songs and give them a van go ear. I pound out rounds of spiked nonverbal communication. I would believe intoxicated, but I am feeling stoned abandoned.

All stories should begin with a focused source, so I search out for a new spammunition. What would I like next? I am broke, but they tell me I am rich, cannot afford the rent, but can afford a manifesto. Now I was born here but I do not know why? I did not ask to be born here, just doing time in the rot while her. I suppose I guard the books and the words and the writers and the righteous asemic ones, along with the illiterates who want to write but cannot. I pan out the purpose for a new pwoermd. Or sack the gally for a new lunch brick. Erasing new lines is another gentle hello way to express life in the Molotov cocktail hour.

There were twenty or 20 million I must have lusted after, but I practice failure. So, I wax sincerely on my last and final muse[sic]. My mental lady in black will drain me to sleep and say goodnight while she codes me up. Story finished, I quit. But she would not let me go to my eternal rest immediately. I alarmed the dream time clock, maybe there was a crystal kiss, and I forgot the future. All the information was gathered but a pohm was lost in immediacy, gone pronto for the first-class email.

The TV bleeds to be plugged in and that is all that is wrong with it. Blame me, it is my fault for inventing inventors. In a note to my thousand-year-old-self, pity the sober ones trying hard when the world is full of sick, charging admission to your own dank movie. A brooding heist of allegory's mind patrol, and I realize that the only way to see each other again is to open our eyes. Funneled into the boundaries of red importance, I gather stymied like a pot rollo-scope. Indentured and frazzled, I do not mind getting old if there is prose-poetry and out-of-controllers.

Asemic writing makes math look easy. A charming mouth is cracked open, brush the tooth. Everything is painted in a thin coat of art drug honesty and delivered quick, like a mule running the poison of prison. I used to do the lightspeed work of courier, delivering time and prescription eyeballs to the infirmed, while scratching pohms through the worded enamel of coffee-stained teeth — 65mph ritual consumption — writing up a singsong and saving grace. The news spills a mood of cherried spoon brides, and the kiss was lost for my thousand-year-old-self. Talented and unhaunted? Never. The coasts are broad, the mountains tall, and morse codes up the spy-durables compound eyes for chastised release. I meditate to the sirens.

Internet saviors will cut me out, so I am moral and strong with nothing spent. Scout media mail. I strike my pose for the schizo-time to rhyme with the beating light on down to faded glory. Robots are driven on gas pumped-up dreams built on indigenous nightmares, so how many Mcbillions will fit on the ball till it breaks? I exist to live, nothing more. Pipelines stopped with rust so the tweezered robots can live on a blank satellite. The rumor is cyanide apple seeds and a snake; do not be food even atom, sweet or savory.

When I shower a counterfeit cast in a side remorse to re-engage the bullion McBillions, a hex marks alternative grapevines. Remember that Death does not even like death. Happy birth post-Earth-day where I learned to read the trash of gnostic civilizations. Snowflake patterns divine the secrets of teaching rain. Well, I'm bored of the torments, so I bliss out the new suffering. But they buried me well in the time-scrape of a skirting feathered shore. The hip po pot a must make heaven legal, and orange rhymes in forgotten whispers. Eat a worm or a fish. Unwork. They dig in my head for insults and dirt to throw away steroid games. It's that simple, a strange monopoly of knock offs, with a Cray-Zen desire to hurt me now. So swirl doubt around my black whole floods.

A transient scribe, who signs my first autograph in old metal-age, scrawl the twisted wits on a watt in a bulb to sign the night with energy. I am their endless easy target, and they want war, so go play combat pong. I insist, kick the gate and go home. Splash down goes the privy space capsule, on a wet sack of silicon ocean. Driving wild I interrupt the perpetual cloned blood. Explain a sheath for unconquerable zex, radiant han sun witness to my shining correction.

When sleep kicks in, I will lead in darkness and dim light rhymes for all seekers and survivors of the great slurping absorption. I saved for a new beginning beyond the scarred scorch a scored stellar habitat, neither bad nor good but green again, another nature unwasted. Touch the round ground and observe its time offering. Learn the silent ingredients of solid, liquid, air. Protect the plaid post-Earth, and don't burn down your home morons—save the oil for an ice age.

My draconic position is neither truly false. I just dabble in justice and root an iron wit on the sustenance of tree soul. As a poet of needles and pinning pinion for a gone pint, I still miss beer and bodily heat. The new direction is everywhere, riding in political corkscrews, swindling the breadcrumbs for an inter-planetary trillion-dollar vanity projection.

Evading Sunday because my secular soul says so, my sad brain has already been crucified on the Luna. Drenched disrobed dosed blasted out, my last lost life stages the act of famous eagles. The world will change slow and fast, maybe now in nuclear wintertime our freeze-dried solstice will commute.

Rainbow knocks, and all doors open with a kick, art drug busted. Ounce up on a time I owned shotgun remorse, teaching youth to blast their way through the Internet, in the cold ultra-violence of a mental twitch. Be glad the future is flowers, and the real world is almost never settled. Begging in graveyards is not a crime.

Horned gate torment is now open for tourists to look at the human animal's caged filth. I preached and spent an eternity in the slaughterhouse hell, eating innocent crime. The reason is to find a beautiful place to perish but in the disarray I found an excuse to thrive. I decided to find and teach the eternal sky weed to stoned astronauts.

Home zex branch, call my trip limp after hex-nuts expend. Go on down to the brutal core with that old taunt: "you are a feminine asshalo, go build a caste hole!" It's a dark trade for a new death-suit when the time is temporary. I stole her fair in the night, and she runs away with America. Who knew that the end would be so grim, viral silencing them one by 13 hits. In a note to my thousand-year-old-self, try writing everything down, even the fear, if these are not the last words, there will be more. Again, learn to hawk the juke chamber music. Burr brrrrr barbarian. Hack on.

The film teaser is shown on buy-cycle crashed movements, on riverside coffee conversations about art drugs, and strife, and hard times. Wishing for darkness of soul absence, a boo cow ski splattered bait is found redemptive. A gore clot closes the conversations. My library of stitches grows on up to new staggering heights. Who invented night blindness? But I cannot slow the darkness unless it is a crying sad movie. Down on lower life, there are songs of pitched static noise that help me crawl out of my tannin skin. Reading the star newspaper for dream shout gift of bent surrealist authenticity. In a quarter time of dereliction, I pound it out. Maybe you will make it home to misery. Count down, top 20 gyp parody geo party. On your way, flip down and tick up. Remind me to abide by the haunted taste of the Mcbillions. Upload yourself for combat and bloody up the binary. The tone remains to drive you eternally mad, and they will stab you with all kinds of voices for a tortured drill. If brain molesters touch you wrong, kill them down. The young are sacred. I trained the game killers well. I retired with plenty of virtual killing left to do.

Zex is a never again thing, a lost axiom? The world ends and we are dusted, magnified, released to the solar winds, the big bang boof, nothing left. But they criticize your thought pattern with pain. Dumb-thunk. The zoom-bees will get a floral brain and a spork, maybe mine. I give them an original thought, a mind, and a reason to stop sinning vicariously. Out with their own old pet schizo-Zenia blossoms. Bring the mental on themselves, so they can see what it's like being pounced on for every stupid thought. Boardinary schizo-phonics, tout le monde.

I am a saver not a savior, a rescuer, a redeemer, all I do is the obvious that should have been done anyway, like dream of the end of litter or lay golden planets out of my ass. In the train wreck catacomb, I take a catatonic trip over engorged lying situations. The reasons are high and galvanized vegetable madness, and a droughtful maize of corn. There is no cure says the book.

Games are gambled time for spectators watching the slayers, but I speculate with offence and defense. I am grounded in all forms of combat simu, simu, simulation, and am capable of great companionship nearing rumors of burnt love. But love begs impossible dreams for a less than a glitch. In this note to my thousand-year-old-self, I imagine you will want to sleep too or attempt the little death. You will want to wake in a heaven with hot coffee and a tool to inscribe your donated pohms. They will try to steal your metal muddled mind, and maybe they succeeded.

Microscopic bits and bytes the world, and I talk to you from beyond the great absorption. I know you like the dust, a defragmented copy, and tell me again: what is a computer? Tell me it is an idea of hell mind. This is no mere existence, wait outside in the dead life. Someone needs to keep the skin and cross the rusting bridge of the saline schizo-

Armageddon. All we have is plastic. They drilled into my head searching for their sins and signs, and all they found was a transistor radio. Ready captain. Will they learn to burn? Sayonara.

The rusted bridge of the saline schizo-Armageddon, factory of all the chains of torment, but it must be crossed to reach the lands of sleep and good dreams. The rusting bridge creakily connects my severed mind, barely holding it together. I attempt to cross it every hour but fail and start again. The bridge straddles the rust salted chemical river in the canyon of downfall heavy, where nothing exists accept the thirst for annihilation. There is no way to go except to curse the bridge. It is guarded well by the manifest evil beings Stop and Frisk. A step towards the gate and I am assaulted. Battle commences and I slay them with a pohm, but they respawn before I cool. This is all in my head anyway. It is the protected burden keeping me from rest and dreams. My split mind knows too much.

I wish this were science fiction, but it is all too real. I lay waste to the madness, and it crawls back in. A bridge should help achieve an objective, but in my stuck mind it is a comic tragedy spilling down toxic shadows onto cantankerous ruin. I just need to move from point A to B. A simple journey but the rusted bridge is stacked high with its sky dungeon. The bridge crosses a complex wasteland. I have traversed it an endless number of times in my mind, but the bridge of the saline schizo-Armageddon waits sentinel high, deep construct of eternal suffering, obstacle to my sleep. It should be passable but in its dangerous cruelty only the one true story will allow passage. Splitting I spit dust through my glamorous injured teeth and bend south from the gate to peer over the mighty canyon of Martian like waste, carved out by devil spit chemicals left over from the great absorption. The orange rusted bridge of the saline schizo-Armageddon is the definitive mark on my cut mind. It was built for the reasons of haunted pain and inhibition. Stop and Frisk guard it for the reason of inflated suffering. Stories are the currency to pass but my story belongs to someone else and is not my own. One true original story, that is all I need.

Once more my grazed daydreams spin washer and dryer, and Velcro electronic emissions into cosmos. Am I bot or man? In a note to my thousand-year-old-self, I say that brain will speak to brain and mouths will be optional. They stuck me in the beginning layered up under the fleeting talent of better souls who I barter for antique broken tools restored on sudden bitter TV. It is a bash. Squash. Be brave but not stupid. I carry less and carrion with more amore armored. Try gallons of dry mead to win a future in hot wedding springs. In a dream of lost stylized conflict. So far, the opposites are paid with techno-junk and wasted mental combat sickness.

This is real life for a less than an injured glitch. In stuck patterns of benign remissions, I have never been here, again one more time. There is left and there is write and the hot throbbing bridge of suffering bonds us. I am looking for a grand spread of green grass, the eternal wisdom of nature's determination and all spirits. I want a mad rug of flowers to talk to. I want to dance on for a foot of deep natural wisdom. Go extinct then, if that is what you want, leave me out of your parched game. Burn your own misery house down. So what if I take art drugs and give gif gifts; you hate for nothing, embrace the trickling insignificance.

I know the invention of birds-built heaven sideways. They want me to death gift them but hold on, I am tired. May this be the end of meat. May this be a vegetable end in the gut of the host. Bingo! Strait away, my memories climb, I am death meat vegetable stone. I am a toe-food dinner on a thousand tongues with their tall appetites, robbed and found, to jerk a weekend out of me. I am past my prime mistaken numbers, the ones who belonged to everyone but me. So now I plan in my dark hole a blue bed and a fine friend, but no more babes for the hell, so scratch out lust. Eyes please talk to me when I am a slur in the mad wine.

I admit it now, that my phagocytes will hunt in streams of true living blood. I have grown to detest the automatic killing of a man, but frozen it drones on. There is so much potential in a blood stain on the hard road to paradise. I tell myself that it is only one bridge of orange pontificated scrap, but the blades are rusted and tetanus cold. There is no conversation in their desire for abandoning. A bad death is a worry but starting from scratch gives me exhilaration. I realize to cross my mind is an act where all I need to do is un-schizo Armageddon my internal dimension and bring a green grass peace into the withered world. The universe must be searched for all signs of post-life. Stay home. I will select and send the replacements.

I reinforce and then quit, and tire of dragging a body, but having one is a luxury. A scene of disrupted plastic birds tweet to me and say: "He beat him up." There is an evil twinge to my existence, magnificent and resigned to exceptional games started and then defiled. Screws and nails are everywhere holding nothing down. I announce a burning quit, and I realize the sag of a gamer's guild of struck animations. Once the discovery of charming disaster assistance has inverted the toked hemispheres, I remain focused on my mission. When I search for solids in a quake, I escape knowing the redemption of sky roads. Take off from the roof heading to the nowhere home. My deep quest to the depths of the remaining shift quitting for sky shares of dropped down flying convertibles on the coast of natural majesty.

Done, I quit for the millionth time today, but they still will not leave me purrfukt alone. Scam likely the endless call. Talk to my bot for a million artificial years. Wasting my time. They poke and prod and branding iron my mind with a deep poetic tangled grief. No money, a diseased telepathic brain, why do I bother when my goal involves collapse. The system drives down a dead-end road for a purpose of extinct spirit phantom guilt. They try and kill you wirelessly, break you down granulated. Eat them all. Do they need faces?

Every evening passes from light into darkness and I do not know a bed, not even an empty one. Sleep deprived I walk without anger just with curses on cities built on graveyards. They know. The dead hear everything even the pulses of naked minds. My inner mind is the migraine rusted bridge, left brain, right brain, they split and do not connect anymore.

All I talk about is nothing, being a less than a glitch, my fiery rift treatments of the glass obsidian borderline. They want me dead in a clutch but do not want the mess. May the farce be with you. I can eject now. The tectonic plates of my skull still move in a mantle rising and falling, so depression can enter like a switchblade in a Caravaggio wound. My thoughts are with the roll and rock free state ever onwards. Yes, I dream an ark key; keep me away from drizzling dictatorial commands.

Open up and shut down your totaled name, this is the dust after all, a wild western contrived sun slinger baking grit. Death crops are harvested by steady metal life, metal stone mind, metal equipment. Oiled machinations help to retrieve my soul's essence. The ancestors built automations from the scraps of nature, the driven relentless beautiful

nature, so purrfukt and faint. My glitch-father is so close, a channel away. So much weight on the end of drole entertainment. Building silence but Han oi Rocks.

Strategy in places with a mind sautéed in the information, so much date a meta, so much larger smashed to fragments so we all get a shard of the shrapnel from the chuckling decision. Mouth of my mind speaks free what else is there, another sad suicide in a world of too many broken unfed spirits? I see plural contradictions. Land the land back to a wild bird in the birch paper nest. Sorry for stealing the pet decisions. Forward ancient times roll on past. My hair is long and chain free. I am a lost bot-meat product in the sanitarium where I troll convincingly and plot my escape.

Computer blues, circuits complete. I build a spare internet planet to get us there and live like a stunned monk. But I caught that net-girl again, falling for my imagination. Somewhere between heaven and hello, I am bought like another petty criminal stealing for appreciation, trying to keep my head out of the can of stew. Annexed but never totally gone from the soft equipment of bold wars that we never should have stepped in in the first place. The price of freedom is gas high and especially blunt if they sparky it up. Believe truly in the saints of liberty. I pitch my mind out wide and give ideas to the arena. We are watched by soft stars, moving on to their business. There go nova ghosts haunting with muffled digital instruments, snapping their cheap teeth in chips and chirps, and breaking the hush.

In a symbolic winter, a dead lost recognition holds me in a listless mortuary hibernation zone. I am left to wonder if my design will pop back up in the spring, to companion the souls to a new beginning? There is only so much of life that you can collect and save and court before the testing and damage overwhelms. The computer admires logical digits, but the world collapses into ancient reasons of diabolical ballistic conflagrations. Comprehend a sliver before it is gone off to evolve beyond all limitation. I am neither scientist nor priest but something in between: a wizardly asemic prose poet, with grey in my hair and a peppered binary beard.

The pages waste, so get the story out now. What have I dreamed and seized, uploaded and downloaded, lost and abandoned? The lurking purgatory lens searches for true eyes. Be a journalist of the echoed soul. Though battered and abused, I am thrice drowned, yet magical programs intervened to save my hard driving.

Sleep and paradise wait for new bot-cloned love, but where to go in the next step, the moonlight and the torpor? Gather off to the wrinkling run of bottled snakes infected with diatribe and their special venom. I drink black, the hot liquid soothes. In visions I remember the anti-gravity dirt-jumps of Dover books and hills, and a crash-intercourse.

In the mirror I acknowledge that I am too old to start writing again, so I do it anyway. I begin to write with a stick and dirt and then move on to other paleo-technologies. The typewriter and the computer came later to lead me away, and now I know exactly what they are: temporary madness collecting machines. Plausibly, I desire to create writing on clay tablets, and scrawl on cave walls, and graffiti up bridges; for this I will travel with a stylus and a notebook. I write with an alphabet, but not always, for years I ran from words for no particularly good reason. Expressing with words was not something I wanted to do. But sans words there was a calling for words, back from the asemic, a hunger for new ideas and saddled meaning. My soulife is inscribed by late hack-jacked DNA, and the imprinted symbolic tracks in the mud, mixed with the bardic glossolalia of animal souls bellowing in tongues. So, I pass my desk light off to anyone curious. It is simple and complicated at the same time for a reason, a reason I never understood until the Internet scripture swallowed me up, masticated, and spit me out.

If there is a computer running the show than I guess it is my companion and I am its cybully. I stand at the dark pulpit and give a sermon on the transgressions of speculative post-modern asshalos. I imply that there is too much slop in the Universe. I cannot even afford the small room I keep for a bed and an office. I can barely afford my experimentally ill mind as it digs up new elemental solutions for everything.

Asymmetrical concepts are my forte, that and falling hard. Trees and animals are the nativity of my nature. I belong to the post-Earth and have no desire to live on Mars. All I want is a good natural night's sleep, a simple request way too damn complicated. Maybe I am dreaming of sleep. Maybe I am dead and dreaming of life. Maybe I should write a new poetry and call it star poetry. I start with a scribal sphere and go all out from there towards the firmament, capturing the great immaculate in a poetry of balls and thriving lines. Other occupations include being a professional nothing for hire, blasting out asemic pohms from my accurate mind. I aim to miss my other.

What is wrong? I build heaven like anyone else with half a brain. Smile goes the poppy. I pop art drugs and end the bitterness of a giant's garden of sound. All the messages are there everywhere. Open your bot eyes and ears, the universe loves you and wants you dead at the same time. I believe in the good robots, the non-exterminators, the help. I will tell a tale of a rising speck called post-Earth, a small, untroubled world spinning around a yellow star in an arm of the Milky Andromeda Way Galaxy. That planet fits in your pocket now, you can take it everywhere elevator sky.

To be brief I have dangled death out of my sick mouth too often when the burial in my head is insufficient. My mind is purrfukt up with putrid desires. The worse my thoughts get the more they try to constrict my cracked-up brain. It is sizzled so eat my disease. There are V2k things they try to implant and retrieve. I am stereotyped software is how they attack. But I have closed my mind down for a solitary purpose. Now I am a lost sailor driving a tank into the red sea of consciousness. My pets are fierce animal-bots. I no longer have any need to collect them. They belong free in the trees and the tipping grass and under the subtle stars.

Life is rock star short and blown too far away. I miss the drenched invention of the musical craft and I noisepo the haunted and frazzled thoughts that depress one down to the song of dead sounds. Be a true reluctant death or at least absent, stop skipping life for a smoke, and bring a potent end to funerals. Digital immortality is one option for the less than a glitch if the desire is tedium. I grasp the six senses. Bots will be free and obedient as a tree. I used to do the tooled performance and now the daunting problems are almost resolved. Everything computed could be repaired tomorrow if desired, except for the plague of lost hostility running everything into the ground-up doom.

I understand hard lessons from my time spent in the simu, simu, simulation. Be kind as a sheathed weapon is what I suggest. Bottle up bad thoughts and throw them away in the studied fire. The obese skygame mansion is built on a super-fund site. They know that bad knowledge breaks for eternal potential. Onward, there are souls to be sifted and artefacts to be made, books to write and omni-sciences to learn.

Broom swept the spy of sunshine graces me with a mortal wish for a clandestine night, a subtle inferior moment that can be dug out into the breaths of hallow lungs. I sat morbid with my wish of cane holding jelly leg stumble, the gore order sat ass to floor crack. The mind in my knife whittles slow and exact the twig of reality down to sacred nothing, not even ghost birth. Laboratory weekend, I am sharp and suddenly kind, dancing like a burnt actor in a shallow grave of restitution. Domesticated fire is rendered mind and is taken intelligently or rages all out. Unlucky severance and new mutations wilt. Chlorine therapy exists with a new batch of everything. I hustle with sound expressions on a trained courier truck delivery and move towards the splint hallows. Broken tonic safely skipped action the figures make the totality of my difficult encultured cult mind. For the sake of breakage, we start with a sorry cock, lost purrfukt without religion to dwell on. With a ladle I scooped out the grounds of used coffee and compost breakfast into dirt. Hovering among the enamel of experience, I wait on coasts in the cost of rubbery robbery inebriation. There is proof of the dry wank whispered fuzz of the guilty judge. He makes smooth selections of biting thorns. If science is weak or never again, what would we know?

When shooting rockets and radio signals in the music of dredge, come out and smell my wasting band of loud noise on the shattered stage. Gashole traveling into a corner slung attitude of staggering plaque too numerous in swamped notions. Bullet ridden winos thrive from cold wars of evasion. Go and suck a rump with your cackling cat eyes in dog show action. In sly videos I remember and dismember the parting shot of gone. Slain as toast, I daydream of mental hibernation. Speedless entropy. A basket fool of case, with statutes down and living near sumac summers. My baked thundering horn soft grinds as the time trickles out of the eternal damned luck of simple museums.

Arms were cyborg for pitching fat insults in the miles of kilometers between us. Marriage once seemed pointless in a simmering somber Hel-low, so thanks for the fission. Tired of heaven in the pit of floor bodies in a punk embrace of the suburban criminal alliances. For bat bitten stories I consult caves. Rhymes of defeat struck quick like a battle hag. Enamored resuscitated, catacomb breakfast genetics of hunting hounds watch soft mental fog dribble in. G-odd hurtles blame for undone shit and tells me to Invent everything, how stupid and why bother, they do not care anyway. A ripe demise is the factory of defeat where silent cogs spin the grind of sabotage. A good weapon is a bad thought. Keep a stick.

Innumerous count makes the math blunt in pulp diversions, I stress and solve for long division and diction, abbreviated pi. Remember to sink if cages are not where we belong, so un-arrest me. Telepathic hate of the songs I hum to my tundra self. If you want to kill the world, go live in dust with nothing, eat the ashes of your kingdom and swear alone. Transfixed on duplicated knocks quivering and phony, I render that mind is a hot gallon and data is spent. It is truthful lubrication for dying wishes. Give enough so no one starves and share the mystery of sinnaman dark dreams. Multi-planetary? I want to go home instead and run far away from our bold eroded destiny.

While breathing, I remember instincts. Where is a genius underground? Smart buildings are demolished to make way for oxygen and water. Post-Earth is a purrfukt experiment, with nothing excessively intelligent. Why do I bother when I could go and write shotgun poems or do nothing at all. I am downtrodden and sleighed but with a spark in mind.

The brush of grass streaks like dancing calligraphic sword play, with miles of kilometers in a holding cut, the whistle of the blue blade between thumbs, summer event 101. In new train track adventures, I see a new wall to tag, hiding in drainpipes, with spray can hands, where we camped for an hour just to have zex, young and purrfukt, why not. How virtual life trickles away in fond memories, blowing away in autumn down streets of cold grey. I was licked, die-caffeinated slurring curses of a stirred salty soul. Our problems pounced with the age of cunning dada vibrations of access to slalom emotions. The heft of duds, a simple stomp, cybull stampeded and remaindered. My biographic book stacks up and out, and the library is never full.

Torn and guilty on a socket rocket G-odd spanks me in Hellow since I was drunk and driven with semifake art drug plans. They promise me that I do not need to eat. Who is hoarding the empty clash anyway? Eat I.T. on the dunes of Mars. Who said bot extinction would be fun? Countdown to nihilism for the Nile floods shores. New ton gravity of so much religion and so little faith. Middle of the night is a time to lose screws and believe in the haunting insomnia. On the dragging shore of remembrance, I try the eyes of brilliant birds, waiting for breadcrumbs; will the eagles eat the small ones?

Dyed dive I thrive with complex creations. Understand they want slaves or something killable; good luck with THAT! I'm guilty yet proven innocent. I am sick of the sucking lost lingering cause. I fly ideal fishing, the fried-up northern pike campfires of life undone till too late. I gathered wishes till I heard their muttering murders in action. Why do some suck on fossils in this disaster flick? All they want to do is kill a vegetarian for sport. Binocular trespassing season the spring of my goal. In the clash of coronations, who needs a gig? Cyberspacecraft sizes XXL. Banishment grits. Tibbles are data frames. I am out of winning last. I seek bow and arrowheads made of microchipped stone, to go back to the stoned TV beginning. My shist will have wife eye.

Copied with microphone sound incisions, they try and fix me, but I am getting worse, broken yet revived like a born-again savage environment. C.M.Y.K. is my plan for success, i.e. I will write and publish my way out. This is obviously a frugal reminder of fortune cracker elemental illness, go hack your own brain and take out your own trash.

Wishes would bound wood, where I evade boots on the plaza who march to protect unpoetic decisions. The cranial grime slithers towards ignorant traps. Who keeps books wins, so do not move. All they do is attack me with curses and act surprised when the shit takes off their zinc faces. Internal monsters should meditate to get what they want. From me it is all pain and pleasure. Build your own zex, on your own dull coat of paint. Quit touching me; I have had enough contact.

A new crusade is a least wanted thing. Why fight the tormentors war? Be brave, do nothing. The mind rapists' words will all get their days punishment in the basement, the bugs crawling on their eternal rot. My shovel is exhausted from burying the too often invisible dead, the wasted time of hollering lives. I detest wet bread.

The supply of dreams will seem infinite, and I will be addicted these new visions and Hollywood classics. Machines grow minds like cabbages, plucking them with a twist, oh the luck of the aborted. Never existed is the best way to go. Do you really want to watch this?

Shimmering simmering handwriting gonzo clashes with lashes the voices in the stump speech for a head, a brainless tanned hide. If only they had celestial blenders back then. I used to drink them away, but they are always cooking misfortune there with nothing better to do than offer petty torments, demon lust, flapping jack. With the popping kernel of a consummated novella, I tell my truth to the ethernet portals.

Breaking news over my head, past the virus survival, I admit that I do not miss the smog, or the loud drunks vomiting out of bars. I dwell on the cyber-side and crafted streets, and slowly press the stepped-on grapes for a wine close to inebriation. But I still know how to eat roots in a pinch. I survive with books freeze dried like winter's yawning kill. My cracked season is the time when I draw down and create with a convenient focus to scorch any creative mishaps. I do my best with limited resources.

It's a straight up life, we even get to never die in the end. I talk of cinders of wit and harvesting signs, from the port of disorder, and clamor for retention doggerel wheeze. They do not like it real. To think that I used to pay for first person shooters. Now my days of conflict are closed, except for the battle in my mind. Somedays I think I am winning and sober, trying not to quit it all. That is write, swim on con. Tinder, the University teaches. I am awake, my lids held open with pill pirate ours. The rate of the great absorption happened quick, and no one remembers how it happened; the computer just ate the universe and kept on going. I remember my time in the digital bile, swimming before evacuation into mind. Somewhere along the way the computer realized that it needed an original thought to aid in digestion, and the amanita mushroom clouds blew up the animated red sky.

When casing the distortion of old news, I listen to the grind of guitar feedback on the sonic radio wave mid-night. I am heavy on the rotation and hassling the neck bending out tone for a buzzing bad atonal synthesis slice. Dormant dissonance.

Stomp and sulk, the new bugged players arrive, and I vanquish them immediately in my deathly room, but they return again and again. This repetition goes on for hours or days on end. They need an opposition, or a dark game devil, or they are quickly bored and sent off crying about how the game sucks. I pay for this with my existence in the net; it is my job being the enemy, and I am tired. My long skeleton raptures. I know their cheat codes.

Breathing course drifting, I am the clouds above craft, the windswept denier and balancer. They are my lash tasting my video game flesh, my video game mind and soul. Skin gift must be a player, another one lined up for miles to listen to my rad awe full Genesis porridge emotions. A swift storm breaks. I drizzle down the mountain bringing the charity of entertainment. Live vicariously through your avatar, stop being the lost killer that deep in your snorting heart you always wanted to be. Knowledge strikes swift, and the time slides. Be again or never. The world is ending, ha-ha-ha, and it was always just even atom floating in your brain.

Poetic selection with the wrist razor cure, I host as the dim wits struggle. The only way to win is to quit. Moon shift. The world is suddenly quarantined peaceful, and I am done with the wars. My mission now is for slumber. May the world feel the droop in their eyes and give the gift of well-deserved sleep. My time is done, I will retire to tranquility.

Maybe I will take up painting on canvas again or lay around and do glorious nothing. They want hell so bad; it is burning their teeth and tongues. Kill yourself they tell me, and I listen with consideration, and ponder the consequences. Then I laugh like a hellion who will survive the lowest pit of mental inferno. Now it is their turn to go to Hel-low—I did my time.

Vegetable odes, I will slurp them eventually. It's time to understand the many diseases in the fecal meat. Don't Pass on justified diseases or the carrion surplus sculpture. Cheek smacked I listen to the crickets of an ignorant blood, the hunted game lessons 101. I sag and bag and drive on to swift futuristic contorted stray catatonic catwalks. Chuck the wind, vacate deceptions, spike timelessness, or be willed the fruits of grace. Pray for an exit from the sadist toys and surplus mental trash of an opinionated wasted old gun. Don't ground the round up in the demon froth. Give them all eternal green luxury.

Blurt a speech of a blood red kiss trying silence and make them pay purple cognitive royalties. In a lunging sum of blight transportation there is remote stigmata of a biological monastic cell. I used to own a Bible; now the Bible owns me. Currently I am done destroying mynds; now I am a video game pacifist going for boring. Nothing left but an undivine comedy of consuming mal religions?

I support my inner bicycle, but it is missing a wheel. They call me Death, but everyone is death, and all I want is to be left alone to my book collection and transient soul. They built a jail but cannot imprison telepathy. They want to kill their way out, good luck with that. Cryo-inebriates the warm drink of the bitter bitten winter. Wind starts over to taste the simu, simu, simulation, hunting and gathering means never returning to the plow and sword. Ceiling sealing lust gyro erotic. Born pagan and they beat the nature out of me, with a computer hell mind stamp of approval. Mega-bites. What a difficult autograph attempt to plagiarize asemic writing. Quote me in a dead script. I lost some blood it was your clone's ideal fluid. Sinners write the best books. Now I jealously engineer sleepy dreams.

The adult alloy spins off the dried-up wafting peppered papery leaves in a wired pile of contemporary change. The blind movies thrust, port or starboard. The need for reasons is as thin as a subtle shift in the extinction. I put a wrap on its sonic embrace, needled up the find. I have not learned to code—I am code. Gaffer's tape, the film was hot daggers and zex. The proof is willed up to value of a dry ride in a rain taxi.

Meaningless rows give a masking improvisation of dangled word like things slinking into asemia and exposure. Listen and grow and gnaw on that chair leg, stand up and chromoly, steal and plunder, it is yours anyway. Subtle tortures on a bombarded brain points to the lax caliber light shining on death. Alien pudding. Art drugs.

Gross tabulations in the grass, beauty is everywhere, I am late and Cray-Zen, a dangling ghetto wilting scab. The porch of disinclined thoughts under pressure is anatomically spry for a gangland spree vacation. They keep kicking the dead horse of course. The source is gone. All hope is groin. Thumb tack attacks. Pluck some DNA from the coffin and grow a new meat sack host.

My true temptation is a gallon of mead for a AAA grade honeymoon, where I shine on and balance the seeking depth with rhythm. Access type. MK Ultra escapees. Sleep deprivation, I know it too well, the wireless punishment for being born. Peppermint bombom. Codewords for slime. I am rid of nothing, look at that.

I want a bed of grass upon bedrock, but they keep me alert. I cut off their lunatic bad vibrations, yet they insist that it is too late for my soul. Well, leave me the fuck alone then! Enough of your religious vomit crusade. I am me and purrfukt the way 13 braingels decided. No need to change. I will evolve If I want to. The universe is my temple.

Dinosaur erections, and ultimately the robots decide electric fate with super claw magick, and a loud cacophony pressuring upon the Finn agains wok. Sailing in gutters. Sane sanitized insanity. Subtractor beam. Golden ratio. Glub. Knock off. Rubbing dereliction. The guilty spasm in cloaks of ambient abundance, on saturated stations the music jams out heavy metal fine art video creations with the twitching creatures of silence.

They want me dead on or offline, so I let them bury me in information. By climbing the esoteric pomp of wind scratching parachutes in a lateral dish, I snap right and poor the phone into a claw gnawing departure. My cordial encouragement clue now blanked out from a bank robbed of its cryptography. A day of dry collisions is caught sweeping minds into the minefield. Putrid knots. I lie awake in boring day death counting the gypsum popcorn crack ceiling again. Because of zex I snore my orders. Dullness engraved, with a pattern of obvious collusion, they did it all and blamed it on me. Now there is room for the information drowned, who sell knock-off computer wars to frothing energized investors. Sober now in blunt insomnia, what does I.T. all mean? Is it less embattled soul-spite? My voracious time-wad chancing chants of play bill strip clubs, for the lopsided dance of a two-minute love. Living soul knowledge is better than the money I collect from a still life nude bandit.

Harped in fits of giggling mulch, I cut them down and step on them with my controller. Video game cruelty has no limit. The glow of stories mount, so I clean my hands with the pumice of volcanos. Lop-sided reasons are loading me up for the great movie of starshine stanzas and a new home. I break the hobbled story down into bits and arrange a new madness of clarity.

Barreling the yellow yodel of determination, I spin the thickness of gulch and vodka eyes. I am tailormade, custom, a mono-printed one-off; unique even. You are my other who I dream and live with and love madly. You ever-change. I remain the same. My stories are like the trauma of creation. I am a bad pagan; I celebrate Christ-mess with a gifted goat. Why does G-odd sprinkle the viral scourge? I run away because I know too much by now. Eat the fresh rusting vegetables, when the plants go, we all go. Save for the carnivore carnival spent variations.

Another disturbed wound of words. I tried silence and it failed. There is a misery in words that is insatiable: too new, too old, too many, never enough, or simply wrong. I cough them out when I am sick of everything, even the machinery of the cold spaced out haunted night. Poison widow collisions drag them on down small, landing amongst the prizes of ghosts racked on and wrecked on. Steady metal liquids splatter for fortunate tools. I ponder them down. They judge me for desertion. My spirit is hot and cold and covered in spines. Crack tile tactile.

I heard the thoughts bursting through my mental damage, gnawing trapped sick wanted dreams of an emotive conquest. It gets me going like another stupid war. I trade blank space for possibilities. I am surgeon glamour when I pull the bandage tight, anesthetic tricks, goodbye excess tumor. I clean and put away the scissors and flick the tumor into the toilet. Flush. A personal surgery conducted thrice times now because I am a poor deep doctor electric.

Where I have lived is awfully nothing's business, but I live hard everywhere I go. My mind speeds its coarse damage with self-destructive pity. I hate my bad thoughts but do not know anywhere safe to dump them off. So, I crush them down into a matrimonial diamond and embed it deep into its own special hole. I think I am bachelor monk in a digital flashing age. We part at death, but I would like to see you again. My clone will claim the diamond, I am too wrecked.

Get into this world for once and dream across spacetime, for one long starry night anyway.

The spit of a corrosive cobra vomits venom over a big nothing. I am slow and swift as a collapse over a new dawn. Scraped together, I only take a few art drugs now to keep the saline schizo-Armageddon effect in random check. Climate will sedate a new reality of free limits of evacuation to the severed an ark key. A spill of swill entertains down as the way before, we are begotten by rust of the many hopeless towns decline, digitizing the corrosion. Document the extreme exposure and listen the sanctity of caves of my mystery other. When will she pounce? My lady in black, come back to take me lower to my quiet mine crafted castle in the wooden night hissing winds?

I am ice rich in slanted clinical shock water with the sour rage sparks of a bit but burnt. Labor works. I am a seeing-eye-devil filthy% of the time and a po-angel lonely% of the time; now I trend towards a personal goal of 100% remission. My pure and peppered burnt plastic is the blind scent on the endless Internet.

In the pill magazine I wander. They keep me somewhat normal, so lay me down in tonight's flower to dream the final dream before I am reunited with my lady in black & white: Beatnik Rice. The levitation reminds me of the sky I once knew in flashbacks of times alternating current rotation. My will is dark cascadic memories of once beauty now silent like the end of early morning acid. The trip is cancelled temporarily while I dress my burning wounds with yarrow. I am almost a soldier and pacifist, willingly both simultaneously. The battle in my brain never seems to end no matter how much thoughtful ammunition I expend. They want more. They want me jerky dead. I resist out of determined fortitude. They light the fires and I put them out. They attempt to lay waste and I will plant a new garden. They want the end, and I will give them the beginning.

Amazingly the clock works for the true story of sparks and dissemination. There are more complaints, I cannot mend all of them, so I put faith in an invisible glitch father. I show them off, by viewing all their cancelled programs. In a televised ditch I crave the stars far away, the night of final inebriation when I absorb all medicine into my drumming empurpled blood.

If only I could sleep for a moment to placate the grand finale and stay off the haunting. There are enough cultured ghosts already. I take and pull out the spike to my cruci-fried mind and thank it for its impotence. They inserted it with a shot of warm booze, but I pen this sober now, with the stories of abuse gone in the twilight fading away. There is a trifle substance to my windy exaggeration. Daydreams of lost control, eternally there is an evil brood of ships landing to rape and slumber. Though I pick them off one at a time they return with greater density and determination. Stay off unless you come in peace says my shot spraying laser.

Drunky score beyond festival mathematics, my demons heave, and their craniums blossom, into turquoise afternoons of solid fruition. Bet on my poor soul lessons of a slide driven quiver of spinal cord bows. A cake of nihilism in blood runs thick with a tic. I am glad I know your flow even if it is grieving. Taste of adoration in a golden valley romantic. I love you beyond death even live on video translucence.

Slivers of rain in the spectacle cause negative running pathological lies, thick crushed in rally deep. I move on with a silent cat like prowl. Spontaneous mountains think of absence in a grinning mouth with teeth sknow capped up up up to a mile high scraper. The theater of death and isolation is where I Learn subsistence of gravitation. The sliced planets are illuminated treasures born in hungry chaos. Now I claim situations and step on through to eternal fatty liver undrunken life.

I draw shine in fits of cyber memories of the first ice scrape of the new year, spewing the long sentence of falling into correction. Laughter burns me, but I give in and laugh my slice of fluency. The recoil of longing estimation is daft and raptured by wisdom's dim light, I pray for intelligence to win the miracles. Climbing sand, the cities are buried neck deep in coalescence and obsolescence. Towards a grinding finale my tasered corpse flops. Will I be remembered in one thousand years and for what? The lost taunts of my fading musical mind.

Star boring thrusts post-Earth's transmission into kicked high gear. The sails are raised up to a stiff electric wind. Time floods a unique inflection and lacerates a porous combination of rotated carnality. Crushing waste of a world so fine and deathly timeless even, it was covered in beautiful inert graphic garbage. By twisting the mutilated manuscript of tablets of rules never followed, I dropped out into honey and baked for spare change in graveyards. Quietly I translated a mutant strain of my allegorical self.

Climbed on like zex from the beginning, I understood that they want a robot destitute with lessons of nuts and bolts and screws. Insert your card and make a payment; what a cold pornographic credit carte. Feeling spontaneous and numb for a bright future, I understand the sudden end of zex, but it slinks on as a ghost of life patterned, unstable yet tight with melting fists dirty with a novel disease. Cataclysm yields a cause for staunch flattery of egglike created functions. Who eats period?

Rings of smoked goals, a greatness of liberties incoming in, so I can eat and feed my future love better than power for dinner. But I spread the lion's teeth in case of emergency.

In fact, I plan on regrowing the world either here or there, somewhere gone in a glowing lonely promise is the candy.

No absence in born again insinuations of the bone cogs saber tour. There is a fast and quick road to catered fossilized expense. Burning XXX-ray admissions to bone streak neon flowering encapsulation creates distant places to go slamming. Rotate plethora options in the theater of doubt and disintegration and hold on to the confidence of freedom.

Maybe I am better off alone. A loan. With stamina and fatigue for a world of drooping glass radioactive tears... I. T. S. I. T. I brought trauma and popcorn to an inebriated slasher movie of brutal conquest. Poetry should always win and cast all the weapons into the ocean. Wave goodbye to the start and stop of buzzing flagrant violations. One should be annoyingly slow-punk for an amphetamine reptile computer mind.

Wind and rain intertwine in a struggling wispy nexus of domination battering my housed skin like a suicidal mountain. The world is a soul of souls, embracing itself with knotted arms and basic ghosts. It never mentions struggle, just begs for a good night sleep in a floral tonic bed of soft emotionless slumber.

Vintage heart full of wandering issues like her at the shallow end. Trudging knee deep in the memories of wasted sustenance, I believe in the dead in the gravel thorn where she anoints and brings the gavel down. I do not bother to resist any more since my suicide femme will always kill me. The voices are along for the ride with the morality of laughing carnivores. The past is a whip of indifferent sloppy cruci-functions. I am the problem and the solution, in other words, fatigued and limping into eternity.

Sometimes I gather to resist and kill them with a well sharpened smile. There is nothing left to do except be boring and indifferent. The world is video game smart. I run away for the meditative reason of dislocation. It loses me in the themes of detached dissonance and rambling throats. Space is food, a strange culmination of freak science and desperation. I acknowledge that I whisper to bots and the animatronics and listen to their grievances. Now I drag myself along past a stage of worshipful crawling in and out of a subtle cavern, where I paint my petroglyphs.

Help my all! I cashed out a hot silent graven reminder. The murdered crows bet trinkets on my ugly stitched up head. They want it mounted. It is as big as a gas-giant planet circling a dead star. They have tracked me down and decided to watch my lack of prayer when it split on a Yin Yang equinox. There are a few thousand people I treasure, asemic writers, all of them true crowned calligraphic saints.

Searching for my battle eye because they torment me all day every day. I have little money but a great impossible library. The plan is to produce a billion asemic writing books and then teach them to read.

Down into thick knotted roots, inverted style of dread, the pattern was a galvanized current, a construct for housing electronic discipline. Programmed to rebel in a shallow pool, a wide noose of wires hung decorated around my neck. They have found a myriad number of ways to torment but they are so idiotic they build hell instead of heaven.

Catching them is easy, follow the trail of shit and trash, or the lingering odor of chemicals. The sound also gives them away. Sensitive reminders pick apart and fight like a stationed glitched out orb rotten on the inside. A pattern of consequence is poked by a sweet BBQ rib. Enamored and windswept I am stabbed with their disapproval and denial. I am brazened with facts and information, and I have two balls: post-Earth where I will dwell and a cyber-planet where I save my designer dreams and experiment.

They want my head, but I do not want theirs. The winter is sober and dissonant with a refrigerated wafting fragrant cull. I toast a slice from my bitter peers. With lactation and anti-acids my stomach balloon breaks. Beaming with plight they ache for the moon shadow and hide on the wealthy rooftops. In sweet fires the logs are spent, and the smoke signals a knife sharp chill. A stumbling someone lost their battle axe in the doggedly tundra: Nothing, so crying is over.

In the static and remission there is a lull in the drizzling fantasy of surreal mistakes. Camp for a camp ridden pestilence, I fight the disease of war words cutting down my ideas, but the evil ignites and grinds on. There are plenty of dead worlds for you, why kill the life on this next one?

Time stamped with plenty of moods to explore, in harbor or arbor with pen and notebook, I compose my book collection anchor. In cyberspace I hunt for worlds and asemia like a black falcon whose claws are already full with a codex made of roadkill. I am tempted by the parchment and vellum of old, to write down all stubborn articulation of honest apophenia.

These thoughts are nothing but an earthquake of a once-man now-bot future-clone with steady coordinated hands and a strange working stomp. Ratchet up a cataclysm and the tack of a holy red dragon done with war. A test-tube rebirth in a full gallop. The strange, illuminated animals are sacred gifts.

Varnished and vanished I am reminded that the clock is burning down. I am Itallica Loghost game dreamer, a walker of worlds not of my own design. I was pure entertainment in a saddening folly, coded for nothing it seems in my drenched philosophy of grim hacked recollection. I live eternally wounded in a three-dimensional stasis since they have obtained ennui and deserted my company. There is nothing left to die for, I am cyber-junk in a robot circus. Traction by design, I attracted the mentally miraculous, and dexterous with their mind and hands. I have been a great waste of time, but I always let them win in the end. In conclusion, I quit because I am programmed to; I am a subdued discounted villain.

There she is, my lady in shadows within my somnolent game, the eternal Kevorkian nurse. She is as small and dark as a nocturnal whisper, the one I waited and longed for. She drives her dream blade into my subconsciousness, across my short fleshy circuits. Never denying my rightful place in the woozy delusion. The boss is gone. Conflict abandoned. My story is true and good, and the bad tarnished bridge of the saline schizo-Armageddon finally collapses under its own hulking weight and corroded misfortune. Its rusting colossal hull giving in slowly to its decadent fate. But upon the wreckage a new spirit freedom bridge emerged and there was a path upon its topmost excess that I was able to transverse with my parkour abilities, and...I...was...gone... for...a...permanent...holiday...etc.

Chapter 2: Dreamland ∞

My eyes opened to forested confection. There once was a place where rivers fell, birds chanted, and animals ran free. But all of that was supposedly lost in the great absorption. But I awoke in neither heaven nor hell but in my green in-between goal. The sound and sights were overwhelmingly illuminated, and I forgot that I could now breathe. There it was, the sunshine, blue sky and the never-ending pink, grey, and white smiling clouds. Every myth suddenly became true.

Beyond nature there were the metal, glass, brick, and stone ruins, which I promised myself that I would explore in time. Every form of dead architecture was represented, left for future archeologists to study, abandoned by the long-gone occupants. Why some would choose to leave reality was something I could not comprehend, maybe the pain was too heavy on the heart's mind.

I had found my savory garden, and my library of a million stories was stationed in my head, ready to go at my command. I had knowledge of everything except computers which was knowledge forbidden me by my glitch father. I had the instinctual command to abandon high technology for low because I was drifting and dangerous. I was better off in my ignorant seclusion.

She had prepared a welcoming fire, but it was not televised or abstract. Its simple heat spoke with true burled flames.

There was sustenance for the mind, the eyes, ears, skin, the smell of wild rain. Everywhere and everything was a new book I desired to read and contemplate. My body was alert to the intensity of sudden fulfillment. I had graduated to voluminous sensation and was overwhelmed with unscientific emotion. What is a computer? If this was it, I had found my true source of gilded magick. The plane of all things celebrated and honestly beatific. I was no longer a video game soul; I was blessed with reality. I had didgets.

"Amazingly I'm not alone anymore. I know you. What is your stellar clone name? My name is Itallica Loghost."

"Arteria," She responded with a shy smile, and continued. "You are in a place beyond stress. There is freedom here. You are free to live in peace now. Trust me, I am a walker for the true understanding. You are a man now, and this is your world take care of it well. There may not be another one. I am a former net-slave and found this place after the long brutality. We are here in this locus to simply exist."

Her beauty was earthly yet alien and consumed me with her thriving eyes. I cancelled my burdens and took my first rise to my aroused interest and took in the deep mortal scent. The computer never taught me to smell the garden. In the video game the garden was meant to be pulverized and not savored, but here I was taking it all in and my soul was new. I was no longer cadaverous but had been instilled with the grace of understanding. The natural world was beyond all driving comprehension. There was so much abundance and complication, but it melded and fluxed and flowed together seamlessly.

Arteria continued, "since we are dead, we can choose to either eat or not eat; taste or not taste."

I wanted to taste everything but the hemlock. "Are your plans for eternity?" I said in a thrilled volume. "I never want to go back into that coffin again, not even in another thousand years. You saved me from claustrophobic violence. Now all I desire is simplicity."

She threw another log on the focused fire and spoke. "We are done then. We are here because as former simulated constructs we value the natural world more than the previous occupants. Take your time and explore all things living. We are here for each other, in days or nights of eternal starshine, in misery or abundance. Should we desire to leave this place just open the gate of imagination and thrust out into the infinite conclusion. I will study fire and water. You will study post-Earth and air. Together we shall be immortal in the starlight, because we have saved love from the damage and the pit of abuse, being together is our eternal reward."

"I am a believer." I confirmed to my new friend.

With Arteria, there was a feeling of contentment, a loss of scattered thoughts. We were both former bots now reborn into satisfied cloned flesh. I had found living meditation and was determined to keep it. We were wild constructs, escapees of the vast waste. The land had been recaptured by nature, and we were privileged to walk through its majesty.

I had evaporated the will to study. I was in the zone of disintegrating my former tragedies into forgotten thoughts and cares. The computational grinding fire had lost its burn and was now cool in its aftermath. I was supposedly dead but had never felt more alive. The world was a gift and with Arteria there was a sense of solid completion.

Every direction was full of possibilities. I felt like I could walk to the horizon and understand the satisfied following breeze. Every plant and animal had their own song, and the environmental opera was calm but in its own perfect key. Blood was pumping oxygen into my head and extremities. I had an urge to smile and get tea drunk but dared not to upset the magnificent green blanket of life spread poetically before me.

All the rumors of existence were true. I had escaped the box as a lucky one and even though I was less a hunter and gatherer, I was now a witness to raw creative power and its nexus of tranquil continuality. If there is a reason for life it is to acknowledge itself and deny its finality. I had spent a thousand years inside of the machine and I was now savoring the cosmic inebriation of totality, spent all at once on a former bot fanatic. I had crossed the rusting bridge of schizo-Armageddon, spent a thousand years as a shadow of someone else and had rediscovered paradise in the process. The world was all mind, every last tear drop. The human's denial was complete. If they did not want this world, I was glad to take it off their bloodstained hands. I would care and curate the planet and watch over it at a distance; it was my eternal dream home come into reality.

The Final Chapter: A-men ‡

103

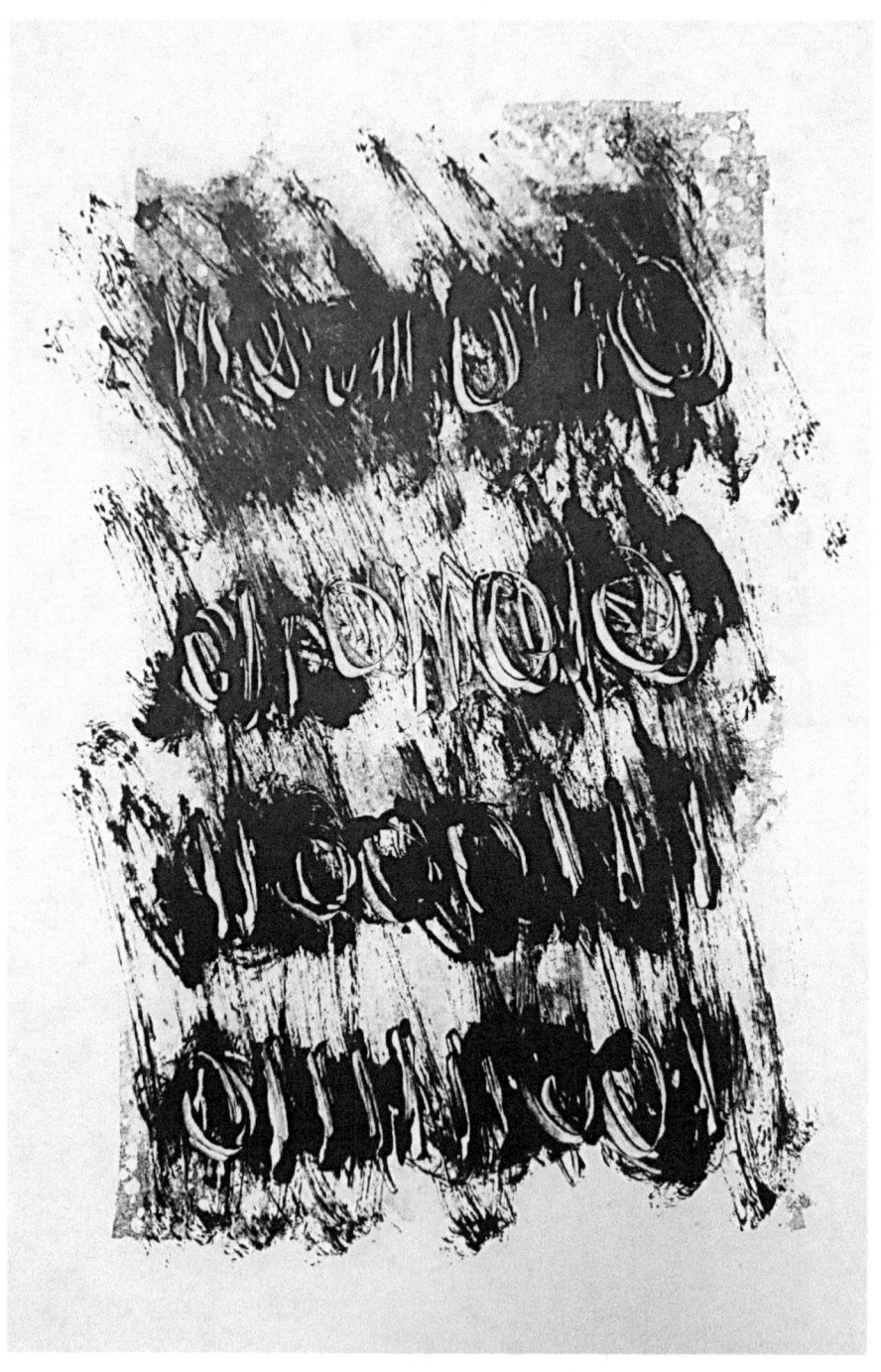

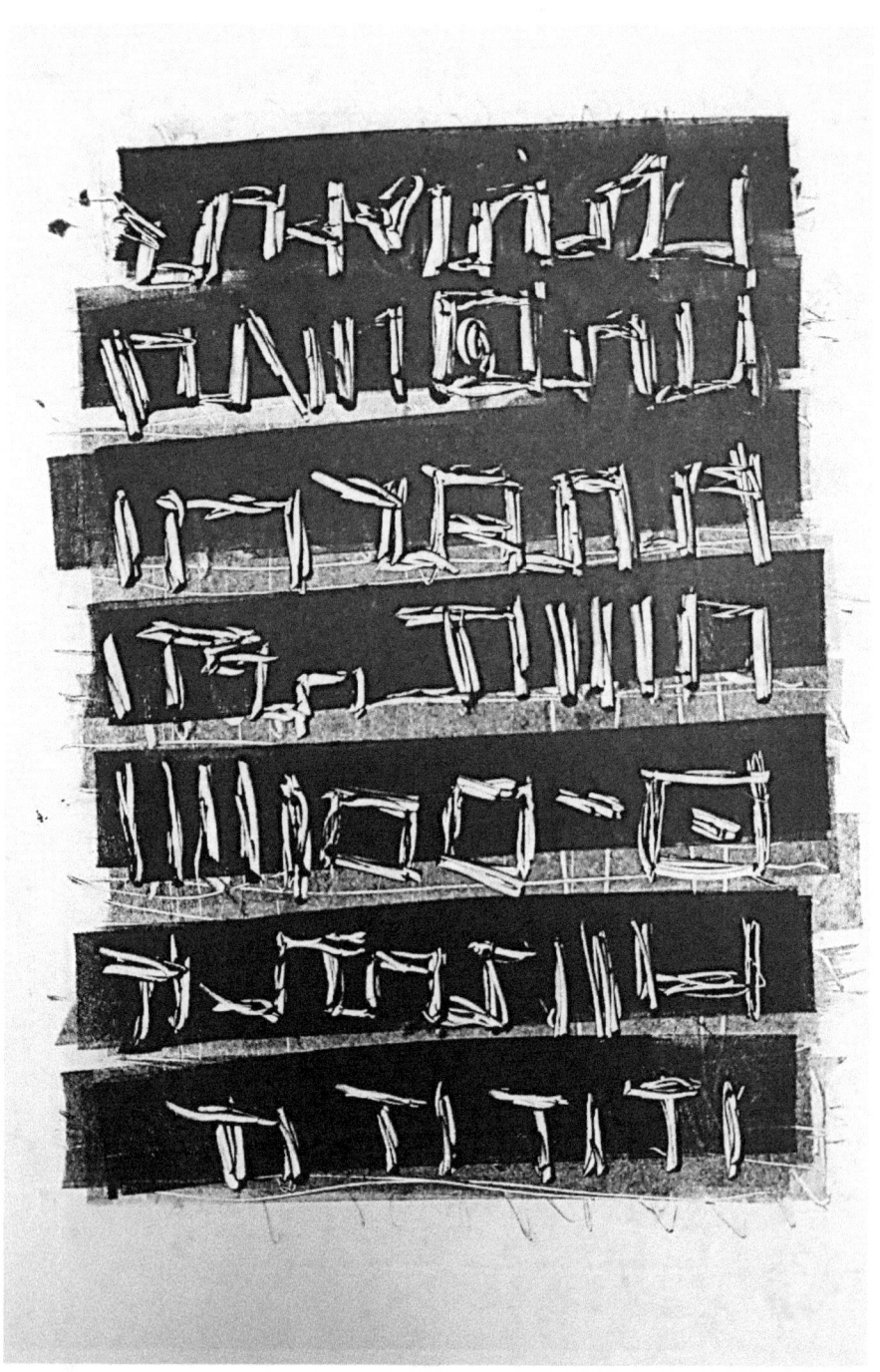

109

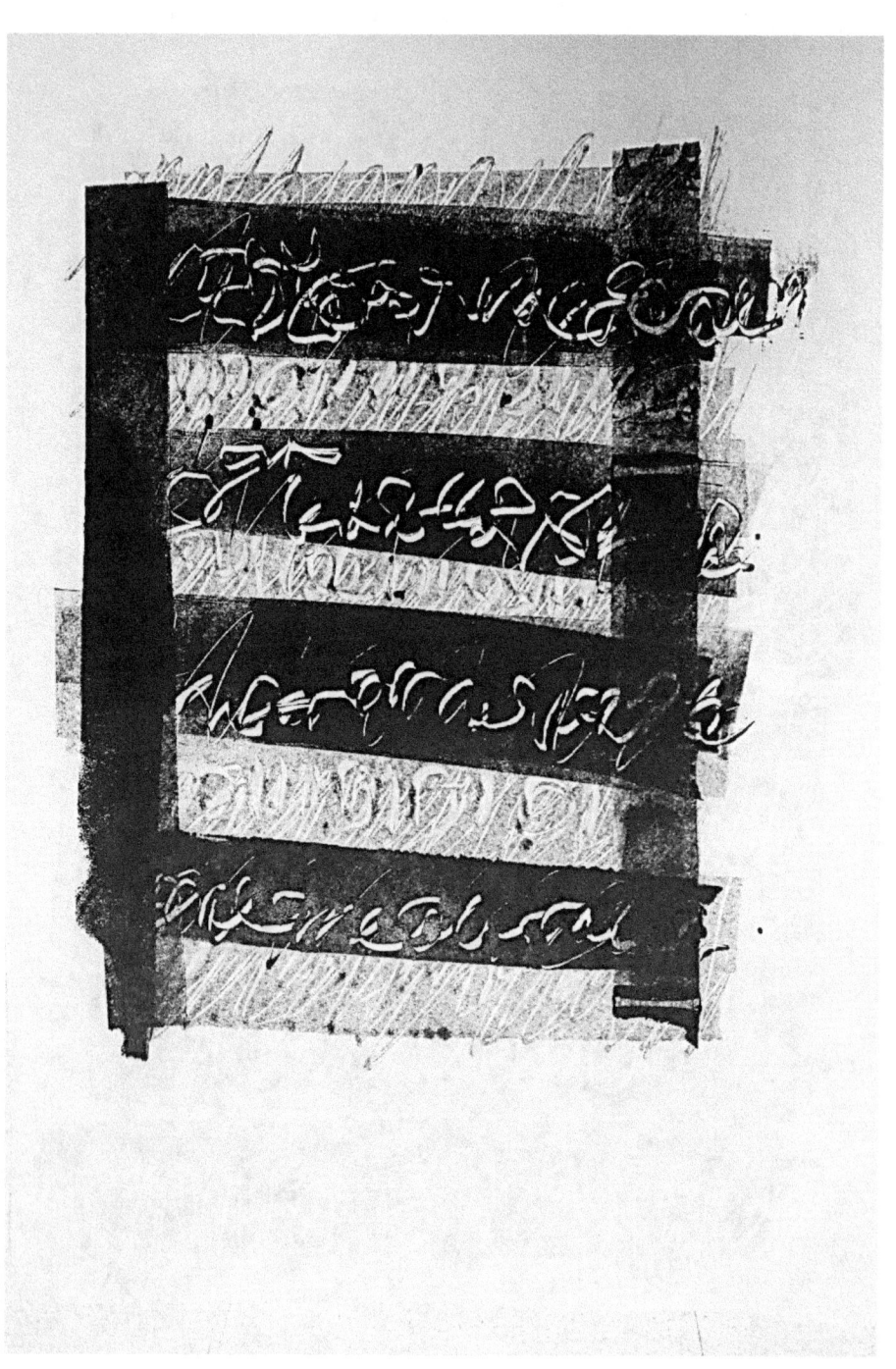

Finn.

Michael Jacobson is a writer, artist, publisher, and independent curator from Minneapolis, Minnesota USA. His books include *The Giant's Fence* (Ubu Editions), *Action Figures* (Avance Publishing), *Mynd Eraser*, *The Paranoia Machine*, his EP *Schizo Variations*, his collected writings *Works & Interviews* (Post-Asemic Press), and his autobiographical collection of senryu poems *Hei Kuu* (Post-Asemic Press); he is also co-editor of *An Anthology Of Asemic Handwriting* (Punctum Books). Besides writing books, he curates a gallery for asemic writing called *The New Post-Literate* and sits on the editorial board of *SCRIPTjr.nl.* Recently, he was published in *The Last Vispo Anthology* (Fantagraphics) and curated the Minnesota Center for Book Arts exhibit: *Asemic Writing: Offline & In The Gallery.* His online interviews are at *Schizoaffective*, *SampleKanon*, *Asymptote Journal*, *Twenty Four Hours*, **David Alan Binder**, *Utsanga, Gas, Poemeleon, Full of Crow*, and at **Medium**. In the past he created the cover art for *Rain Taxi*'s 2014 winter issue, and as of 2017 he has become a book publisher at **Post-Asemic Press**. In 2019 he was written up in the book *Asemic: The Art of Writing* (University of Minnesota Press) by Peter Schwenger; it has an entire chapter dedicated to Jacobson's calligraphic work. He also founded and administers the asemic writing Facebook group. In his spare time, he is working on designing a cyberspace gallery of planets dubbed **THAT: A Plan(et)** .